Tom and Stomachi

Simon Andrew Sheeran

Yolanda,
Thanks for
porch times,
— Simon Sheeran

Contents

Part One

- I -

The Thing in the Desert

Tom awoke, like so many other times, on the belly of that fearsome Thing. He was awakened by the shaking, which was followed shortly by the deep grumbling, like explosions in a vault far underground, through which, try as he might, he simply could not sleep.

As he awoke he knew that he would need to begin searching, like countless other times, for food for the Thing whose shaking and grumbling were becoming increasingly violent and foreboding. Luckily for him, though, he saw a piece of unidentifiable stuff lying on the ground, a scrap left over from the night before (at least he thought of it as the night before, although he had no sense of day or night in this place). As always, he had been exhausted, he thought as he bent hurriedly to pick up the stuff and toss it into the mouth. Far from quelling the grumbling, the stuff summoned forth from the mouth a deafening damp roar, followed by a sticky thickness of a humid poof of wind, which he could only imagine to be a belch. (This could also be called a miasma.)

"On I go," said Tom to himself, beginning to hop over the rippling, quaking belly beneath him. The flesh was wet, and hairs wide as snakes lay matted upon it, making walking somewhat difficult – not to mention the motion underfoot. He slid and stumbled his way down the side of the belly onto the ground, sometimes gliding on his backside.

He knew it would be all right this time, for he had chanced upon a generous pile of stuff some distance to the right of the Thing the night before, which he had not been able to make away with completely (right, from the Thing's point of view, of course, which was as good as his, which he liked to think of as the east).

As Tom walked eastwards he always thought of himself walking across the desert, which indeed the landscape did resemble, in search of oases or, better, rivers, the Tigris and the Euphrates, of which he had yet to catch sight in his wanderings. The riches, too, of the east he thought fondly to be awaiting him, but somehow he managed always to find a convenient pile of stuff before ever making it that far – convenient, in that he never found it too late, although when he returned to the Thing he returned often to the sound of a feverish mew, or a whimper, or a bark, or a roar – he didn't know how to describe it, but some mammalian or possibly serpentine utterance at any rate. Sometimes Tom swore he could hear the sound of people talking, a person talking rather, although the voice changed so much in pitch, tone, and speed that he could hardly attribute it to one set of vocal chords. If indeed it was speaking voices, or a voice, as he liked to imagine, it was not speaking any language that he knew. At this point he decided that he might be daydreaming.

But Tom knew, deep in his heart, that even if he did reach that distant oasis, or that river, that many-gardened Babylon with its riches, he would still hear faintly though clearly the voice, as he liked to call it, harking him from across the desert, wavering between various tones of entreaty, frantic bursts of outrage, charming calls of song at times, and he could not but return with the riches of Babylon to the Thing.

Tom mulled over this idea for a while, chuckling grimly to himself as he squinted into the dusty horizon, which was somehow shady though free of anything at all save himself, searching for that pile of stuff which he knew to be somewhere. As he chuckled he began to remember his dream, which occupied his mind for a while as he treaded eastwards. In his dream, he was walking through a seemingly endless maze of corridors. It seemed to him a striking contrast to his present environment, which bored him beyond measure: something about its dark blankness disrupted him fundamentally, and stripped him of all sense of time and space. In his dream the corridors had had a certain elegance, never winding but sometimes turning into stairs or opening into vestibules, which made his wanderings interesting. It was true that he could not remember much of this dream besides the little just recounted, but he hoped to remember better in time. He thus contented himself with wondering what it was about the dream that so pleased him, in contrast with his present situation. Maybe it was that the corridors, with their contained and orderly layout, provided him with a reassuring sense of order. No, he thought, there is nothing more orderly than sheer emptiness. Maybe it was that the plenitude of being – of walls, ceilings, floors and the odd staircase – filled his dreaming soul with content. Content is often enough, regardless of type, he realized with a feeling of slight revelation, at least it is better than nothing. And content, he said to himself, is exactly what this desert is lacking. He wondered if there were any such mazes in Babylon. He seemed to remember having read or been told of great palaces there. Surely he remembered it. Great palaces would be more than enough content.

Suddenly he was standing before the pile of stuff, an unlucky thing, because he liked to look away from the piles as much as possible. How he contrived to find these piles without looking at them directly was always something of a feat in itself, but it was just doable as he had nothing against looking at the piles from a distance. Closing his eyes, he proceeded to grasp with both hands at the pile, feeling with a unique mixture of disgust and relief the dry organic stuff between his palms and fingers. The Thing, he thought to himself, will not want for much longer now.

He stood upright and began walking back the way he had come. Just as he began to anticipate the Thing's growing hunger, he felt the earth begin to tremble, the prelude, he knew, to those perplexing noises described above. There was a moment when he wasn't sure if the trembling was real or if it was his anticipating imagination, but then he *saw* the trembling, in the dark air, the open gloom, a windy shiver, and there was no doubt that the Thing was getting hungry. He thus picked up his pace as much as possible without losing any of the stuff and negating his efforts.

"I'm coming, I'm coming," he said, as if the Thing spoke his language, as if the Thing had ears, as if it would have any use for ears! No, the Thing had no need of ears, as far as Tom could tell; all it needed was its mouth, gullet, stomach, and vocal chords (maybe a roomful of maniacs down there, among other things, to produce that assortment of noises).

Right on cue, a bark of impatience echoed through the gloom and under the closed sky. The bark was followed immediately by many barks of higher and lower pitches, overlapping, interweaving and interrupting, a cacophonous harmony of hounds, almost sophisticated were it not for its overriding feeling of vulgarity and malice. It was terribly frightening! Just when he thought his ears, his very soul could take no more, that he would never sleep soundly again, never again find himself the amused protagonist of some delightful content-filled dream, but permanently petrified, the sounds stopped short, falling over each other into an abyss of silence. Naturally this silence was also quite disturbing.

But the silence did not last. As if only giving his ears brief respite to preserve his sanity for its own survival, the voice resumed its harangue, personally addressed to the only poor soul in this desert, Tom, this time with typical vulgar originality hitting a nasty note far below any healthy register, and holding it, thusly:

"Hummmmmmmmmmmmmmmm ..." and onwards, until the ground began to vibrate and the gloom to shudder beneath the ever-collapsing, dark ceiling of sky. Naturally this was quite horrible, but it was better in its predictability than its forerunner, that terrible, muddled, harrowingly irregular barking. That, he simply could not take. Indeed, who could?

He suddenly wondered whether or not the Thing had a mother. How had it got here? Had it always been here or had it started its life elsewhere and somehow ended up here? Had it ever been self-sufficient? (All this, while he trotted hurriedly towards it.) Perhaps it had had an accident – fallen from the sky, maybe, or been beached like a whale when the waters receded (he had no evidence that there had ever been waters here, but nonetheless he speculated), presumably towards the Mediterranean, *his* Mediterranean, westwards. Perhaps it was a sea-creature of some kind. Or was it a part of the scenery, he wondered, like a tree, with its roots extended far into the ground? But why would it need him, if it had roots? Maybe they weren't roots at all, but some sort of organic chains, tying it helplessly to the ground. Objectively he often felt sorry for it, in those rare moments when he was not burdened with its horrific need as he was at this moment. The thought of this Thing having a mother who once loved and cherished, cared for it, provided for it as he did, and now no more, was accompanied by a kind of melancholia which he felt might return to him at a more convenient time. He wrenched himself from these speculations; but he did resolve to study the underside of the Thing, its back, he supposed, with the intention of discovering how exactly it met the ground beneath – was it attached or not, or what.

He began to see the Thing on the horizon, blurry amid the dark wisps of gloom which flickered about it like a congregation of mourning spirits; and the humming began to hit him directly, a shockwave of discomfort. He flinched and protested; the Thing, as if catching a glimpse of him or sensing his approach, suddenly changed its tune, or its note, and began booming out a randomly swerving melody, which was really quite charming. Like a kite possessed by a terrific wind, the melody danced and bobbed, skidded over the air, never allowing its next move to be predicted, but always beautiful. For a brief moment of what could only have been a sort of madness, due no doubt to his overflow of relief at being so close to feeding the Thing (always a time of great relief for him), he cried, "my Love!" but, as he spoke, as when a dreamer speaks aloud and thus realizes he is dreaming, the tune plummeted headlong into the kind of appalling, fluttery, inhuman chattering which he always found so disturbing. This time it was like a flock of fretting gulls evacuating south for the winter. "Ugh," he shuddered, "it must have been the ... ugh."

As he came within its direct vicinity, the muttering stopped, and the Thing seemed poised upon the point of orgasmic release (or maybe it was the predator's stillness when hovering over unwary prey?). At any rate, it had stopped its noises. Its sense of smell, Tom felt, must be stronger than his; it must smell the stuff, know that it has arrived, arrived for him, or her, or it. The Thing. He knew that it would soon change its tune: this was an axiom, one of the most solid axioms of his existence.

He dropped the stuff next to the Thing's heaving side and, after picking up a generous handful of the stuff, began improvising footholds and handholds (for no imprints ever remained) on the blubber, making his way up its side towards mid-belly. From there he made his way up the chest to the throat, amid the tempestuous, ravenous shaking, until he was at a good vantage point to throw the stuff into the mouth.

After he had thrown the stuff into the mouth, the voices died down and a strong calm came suddenly upon him. Deciding not to fight it (it would be at least a few moments before the Thing would again become needful) he collapsed onto his hands and knees right where he was, on the throat of that fearsome Thing. He slid and rolled down the chest, with the aid of the quaking, until he lay where he had awakened just earlier. It was a kind of groove, a cradle, as he thought, where he was wont to regain his strength; certainly it was the most comfortable place that he had found on the Thing, the place where he was least likely to be thrown off by the shaking and the grumbling. Indeed, it was even almost as if the Thing wanted him to make this place his bed: it seemed to direct him there after each feeding.

The belly was now making the noises Tom had come to associate with what he called digestion, and these noises were of a strange assortment indeed: there were splashes, soft like the lick of calm lake waters on the wooden pillars of a dock; there were other splashes, seemingly in another compartment, louder and more violent, like the awesome claps and hisses of a stormy sea against the stubborn starlit cliffs of nighttime; there were thunder claps, again as from another compartment; behind these Tom thought he heard the voices mingling in approbatory guffaws; there were screams and whimpers, seemingly of pain; and beyond it all was a kind of hum, or purr, which seemed almost to drown out the rest and was very conducive to sleep (this may easily have come from Tom's own brain, but the rest he felt sure was not his). The belly rippled ecstatically, but this did not bother Tom as he took the brief opportunity to rest and, he hoped, possibly recover from his travails, which were always arduous and rather traumatic. He sank further into his heap, himself, and felt the belly envelop him softly like a pile of pillows. Its embrace was warm, loving, firm (perhaps too firm), and thankful; the voices seemed to coo and lullaby him and the vibrations were actually quite relaxing, when experienced horizontally. Before he knew what was happening, he was falling asleep; and as he dozed off, he muttered, "Were this not my own dream, I don't see why I would ever bother having it."

- 2 -

The Castle by the Bay

Tom was transported immediately into a room of some kind, and he was staring directly into a large bright window of gothic style: a large, sharply arched window divided into three medium-sized windows, which were in turn divided into several smaller windows. He was blinded to the inside of the room by a sharp light in the sky beyond the window, presumably a sun of some kind, which left only the rich darkish blue of the sky beyond visible to him. The light was not harsh enough to cause him to squint or shut his eyes as he would in real life (especially so for Tom, who had not seen the sun for some time); they remained wide open as he stared at the sky beyond the window.

He was standing, and he continued to stand there for a long moment as he gazed contentedly at the window. The sight gave him a powerful feeling of elation, and the rays of the sun made his nerves tingle happily. Though he knew he was standing, he felt very much as though he were floating, or swaying effortlessly like a sail in a calm but steady wind. Eventually he began to drift towards the window, out of a natural and unconscious urge to have more light, more sky. He approached it slowly, surefooted, still oblivious to the room itself; he felt as though he was being pushed gently towards the window by a lukewarm wind. As he approached the window, the sky beyond opened up to him. There were soft white cumulus clouds, friendly plumy poofs not heavy enough to gather shadow in their bellies, drifting steadily across the sky. The sun was fantastic, filling the sky with brilliance and wonder and promise. It hovered low, but Tom had the strong impression that it was morning, for there was no hint of melancholy in the air – all was brightness and elation.

After what felt like a long time of floating around, waywardly in every direction, basking in the gentle sheen, he got close enough to the window to see the horizon and, eventually, everything in between. It was a fantastic scene: there were awesome tall mountains at the horizon, cutting darkly into the sky, over which the fresh sun peeked piercingly. Beneath these mountains was a great expanse of dark blue water, a large bay whose waters were rippling in time with his own tingling nerves and reflecting in sparkles minute and innumerable the sun. As for the immediate environs, he seemed to be in a large castle, or mansion, with wellkept grounds which stretched about a half-mile down to the bay; the grounds were irregular, with gardens of various shapes and sizes and structures of wood and stone. Framing these grounds were tall woods, speckled with large fields and villages, which spread over round hills and small valleys. The scene was not busy, but not dead either; Tom felt that things were going on, but not of a hurried or frenzied nature. The whole thing was incredibly fantastic and profoundly impressive, and filled Tom's breast with a heavy awe and made his heart palpitate urgently with elation.

From this scene a movement caught his eye: it fixed upon a figure in the yard just below him. Tom thought that it was a man from his hat, shoulders, hands, and clothes, and he was unhurriedly raking the grass around a small garden beneath a wall adjacent to the edifice in which Tom was. Tom felt a strong desire to go and speak with this man, whom he decided was the gardener, in the hope of getting some kind of explanation from him.

Tom turned from the window, and took a moment to let his eyes adjust to the light inside the room. It was a large room, with a tall ceiling supported by smoothly carved wooden rafters. The room was clean, and seemed full yet not cluttered. There were several paintings of various kinds of landscapes hanging upon the four walls, between which were hung arabesque tapestries of tastefully sombre colours. Whoever lived here obviously enjoyed landscapes, and knew how to fill a room without bloating it. There were well-carved armchairs sitting about the room, and there were desks and chests of drawers upon which sat trinkets – a gold-coloured model of a leopard, a bronze statue of a samurai, a silver jewellery box, a little model aeroplane, and other things – and a carpet of the same arabesque style as the tapestries covered a blue-tiled floor. A grey cat looked at him curiously from a blanket-covered armchair and, hanging upon a wall, a clock ticked quietly which Tom for some reason thought was also studying him curiously. The room was very inviting, and Tom felt welcome to stay for as long as he liked.

Driven by his urge to speak to the gardener, however, Tom found a heavy wooden door in the wall to the right of the window (to the south of the window, if Tom's assertion that it was morning was correct) hung with large metal rings for handles, opened just enough to allow for the passage of a cat, the hinges of which worked smoothly as Tom pulled it open. Before him was a large corridor, well-lit by a medium sized window in the left (the east) end of the corridor which let in the light of the same sun in which Tom had just been basking contentedly. This corridor, though obviously not a chamber of the same importance as the one he had just left, seemed a very comfortable place in which one might spend a lot of time very happily. There was another armchair set just under the window, upon which sat another cat, this one a tabby, and there were a couple desks adorned with the same kinds of trinkets as were in the other room. Tom walked to the western end of the corridor, passing by other large wooden doors, and found a staircase leading down, back towards the eastern end of the building. Leaping energetically down the stairs, Tom found them open into a little vestibule with coats and hats of a quaint, antiquated variety hanging on the wall.

Finding the front door open, Tom walked out into the morning air, feeling his nerves rekindle in the sun's rays. Smells filled his lungs, of seasalt, flowers, forest, and woodbine. The wind was strong, but warm and welcoming. He knew that it was morning and, moreover, that it was springtime; he sensed even that the snow had only just vanished completely the day before. He squinted, as the sun seemed much stronger now, and shading his eyes with his left hand he looked about for the gardener. Seeing him raking some yards away from where he had seen him earlier, Tom walked towards him, slowly so as not to alarm him, for Tom inferred from his stiff gait that he was old and thus perhaps delicate of heart. The man lifted his head and began turning casually as Tom approached, almost as though he had been aware of his presence from the start and had just been waiting for Tom to approach him.

Tom spoke, "Excuse me, sir."

The man, now turned around completely, was indeed old. His wrinkled face was tinged by a softness seemingly bestowed by some profound sort of peace of mind, and he looked at Tom knowingly and reassuringly, a smile growing slowly. Wisps of white hair fell out from beneath his widebrimmed hat, and he wore a light blue shortsleeved shirt under brown overalls which looked old but clean. His white beard seemed to wear the arrangement of a smile.

"Yes, sir, how may I help you on this brandnew perfect morning?"

Tom, suddenly realizing that he had not planned what to say to the old man, grabbed his jaw with his right hand and stared at the man's feet for a few moments. They were in green Wellington boots wet from the morning dew. He registered the man's growing smile. Deciding to appeal to the man's ingenuity, he turned and gestured towards the open doorway, trying to arrange his features into an expression of confusion, and began saying words which he thought might help, "I ... just ... this place?"

"This is probably my favourite place," said the old man; he stood back and looked up at the building behind Tom. Tom turned and looked at the building. It was a large, rectangular edifice with huge arched windows which didn't make much of itself and exuded a calm aura of confident, welcoming serenity. It gave the impression that within its walls rested peaceful dreams, blue skies of restful peace.

"It's very nice," Tom said.

"Don't I know it?" The old man looked at Tom and smiled as though he had just remembered a very funny, happy story. "And the countryside ... the water, the mountains," he looked up as into a corner of his brain where he was wont to store lists, "and the trees and whatnot. Yes." He let his rake fall. "And in this season, at this time of the day, with the sun just creeping up over the mountains. I'd say you came at a good time."

Tom, reassured by the man's mood, said, "I daresay you are correct."

The old man leaned back, as though decided upon something profound and good, and turned to Tom. Closing his two hands behind his back he said, "I am the gardener, and you may call me Peter." He extended his right hand to Tom, which Tom accepted. The old man's grip was a good one: firm but not too firm. "If you prefer, you may call me Peter Gardener, or even Mister Gardener if you prefer."

They began walking leisurely downwards towards the bay, weaving between gardens, trees, garden sheds, low brick walls, and fountains. Their eyelids lowered to the rising sun, Peter began to talk. "I'll tell you something. Don't worry; it is not something sad. That house behind you is a very happy house. Nothing can really go wrong in there. It is a sanctum, if you will, a stronghold against ill; its walls envelop an imperturbability. Its design is an ancient one, and it has never suffered so much as a crack. A truly amazing thing, wonderful entirely." He scratched his whitebearded cheek thoughtfully and said, "In fact, it would be wrong to say that it is a stronghold against ill or anything so silly of the kind, because ill or any thing related thereto does not exist in the context of this house. You see, it is like speaking of colour to a blind person ... no, wait ... it is not quite like that," – he looked suddenly at Tom as to assess something quickly – "but you get the picture."

Tom nodded, interested. It truly was a splendid place, he thought. "I didn't explore it very much. But what I saw was quite nice."

The old man nodded earnestly, looking up approvingly at Tom for a moment before continuing. "It has been here for a very long time. Nobody really knows how long, but that is of little importance. I think you get the point; even though you may not realize it in its absolute fullness now, I feel that you grasp it innately, on a more fundamental level." His intonation was confident, wavering steadily between fifths and halftones, like one who was reciting well-tried knowledge, or even ancient lore.

Suddenly Peter stopped and touched Tom briefly on the left shoulder, startling him a little, to get his full attention. "But now, I must get serious with you. There is this little fellow, about this high;" – he put his hand out to indicate a height a little above waist-level, just over three feet – "I needn't describe him physically to you, because you must never go anywhere near him. If you see him, run. Do not let him stop you. He will call out to you first, because he likes to cajole, but you must ignore him. He will doubtless try to reassure you, and maybe make a promising, even irresistible offer, but you must turn and run as soon as you know who he is."

The old man looked so serious that Tom found it rather funny, so early in the morning, and thought perhaps the old man was playing a joke on him. He crossed his arms and looked at Peter incredulously. Peter returned his look with a reinforced gravity, and nodded once and continued. "He has a kind of rambling croak of a voice, and he talks very excitedly and steadily, a constant croak. He wears an old top-hat and a dirty brown tailcoat. Don't let him get anywhere near you." He looked hesitant for a moment and pursed his lips, then continued, "He has a kind of a big crayon, which he jabs people with." He looked at Tom seriously again, and Tom got a very uncomfortable feeling, which caused him to want to end the conversation immediately and leave. There was something eerie about Peter's change of manner: Tom got the impression, inexplicably but unmistakably, that Peter believed that Tom knew this person and had somehow forgotten of his existence; it seemed that Peter was reluctant to remind Tom of him, but felt it was necessary. But Tom, to the best of his recollection, could not remember ever having met a dwarf, much less of this description.

"Well, sir, I thank you, and I think I might move on now, taking the benefit of your advice with me." He extended a hand. Peter's features relaxed again, and he smiled, causing Tom to feel comfortable once more, and somewhat sorry for having felt uncomfortable with him. But Tom had committed now, and Peter shook his hand, then gestured about at the countryside.

"It is a beautiful place, you know: a beautiful world. There's no room for sad stories in a beautiful world like this. Ah! There's no place for them. The world will be beautiful no matter what kinds of stories we manage to tell ourselves; this is something I have learned from my time tending the garden. Don't forget what I told you! Much depends upon it!" He began strolling back up towards the house. "There's a little road just behind you; it will take you somewhere beautiful, I'm sure!"

- 3 -
The Group by the Stream

Tom, wondering at Peter's remarkable peace of mind, turned and began walking down the road upon which the old man had set him. The road, of the cobbled variety, was gently winding, and bordered at either side by tall woods which threw shade upon parts of the road, and there was often a little house, set back into the woods, with a winding path leading to it through the trees. For the first little bit of the path Tom could still see some of the bay and its surrounding landscape, but soon the trees of the forest hid the water and the horizon and all Tom could see was the blue sky and its unthreatening cumulus clouds. The atmosphere was calm and quiet, and Tom felt that people came here to escape the bustle of the world.

Tom did, in fact, consider at this time that it would perhaps be a better plan to remain in the house, or on its premises, for as long as possible, since Peter Gardener had spoken so highly of the place as a paradise of sorts. The logical extension of Peter's assertion, Tom reasoned, would be that other places, outside of the house's premises, were not equally devoid of unpleasantness, and there might even be some danger lurking beyond, aside from the dwarf about whom Peter had warned him. The foolproof, safe plan, therefore, would be to stay at the house – that is, if Peter would allow him. However, Tom concluded that he would go on the way he was going, deciding that if there were any serious dangers lurking ahead of him, apart from the dwarf, Peter would have been good enough to have warned him about them too.

Tom then reflected that the interaction he had just had would have been a very pleasant and reassuring one had it not been for that bizarre and somewhat disturbing warning which Peter had so seriously given him. However, Tom thought, there is no kingdom in any world that has not its felons, and it is important to remember that. Perhaps Peter did not want the extreme beauty and overwhelming wholesomeness of this place to cause Tom to let his guard down, or dare to think that everything in this place was perfection. Perfection, Tom thought, like that house, for instance, if Peter Gardener can be believed. Or perhaps it was just the gardener's nigh senile fondness for a place whose garden he had tended for a long time?

After passing by a few houses on either side of the road, half-concealed by the trees, Tom began to hear the unmistakeable sounds of a stream, to the left of the road about twenty yards along. As he drew nearer to the sounds, he began to hear voices. The speakers sounded youngish to him, and he wondered if it was a good idea to reveal his presence to them. Deciding to leave it up to chance (for this had been his strategy so far) he continued down the road until he reached a point in the path where he could hear the stream clearly and make out the words of the strangers; he was separated from the group only by a handful of thickly grown pines.

"I always find it ... remarkable when one turns up alone," said a young boy's voice.

"Well, she's had a hard time, Ronny," a deeper voice replied.

"She's lucky to be alive," said Ronny, in wonderment.

Here a young female voice intervened, "I don't like her."

"That is not at all important, Calpurnia, you know that," said Ronny dismissively and authoritatively, although he sounded young, certainly younger than the other boy for his voice had not yet deepened. "I have never yet known you to like another member of your gender." Ronny spoke confidently and intelligently, a little haughtily even, but the effect was sometimes undermined by a crack of the vocal chords which betrayed his prepubescence. There was, however, an undertone of good-natured humour, even satire, in his reprimand, which made it seem as if his petulance was only in jest, and also made him seem mature.

"That's not true. Oh, look, she's crying!"

Tom began to feel that this group was not likely to harm him, perhaps not even capable of doing so. Leaned up against a tree he waited and listened harder, just to be sure.

"It's been a while since we've found someone. There were those others, but ... that was different." The other male was older, a teen or young adult, and he sounded, if certainly not stupid, possibly simpleminded or shy; his voice had none of the assertiveness of the younger, and was also strangely devoid of guile.

"Yes," said Ronny, "I know. I sometimes wonder if there are any at all ... but of course I know there are, all over the place probably. Not that we want to meet any of them, of course."

There was a brief silence, then the older boy sighed. "Well, let's bring her to Mother."

"Why can't I be Mother?" Calpurnia asked in a supplicant whine.

"You already know why, Calpurnia, and we all know what you'd do if you were Mother."

There was a pause, and then the two boys laughed; there was a particularly unthreatening, almost comic counterpoint in the sound of the pompous, high-pitched voice and the guileless deep voice mingling in laughter. "You can be Grandmother if you like," said Ronny.

"Shut up, Ronny," said Calpurnia. "I'm hungry. Let's go!"

Tom, finally completely unafraid of the company by the stream, coughed loudly and began walking through the thick pine division.

"Look out!"

"Whoah!"

"Who goes there!"

The three cried out at once, and Tom heard shuffling. By the time he made it through the pines, he met with a sight which he had not expected: a short, skinny boy pointing a revolver at him, and the other three, two of whom were much larger than the boy, huddled behind him. Tom immediately put his hands up and cried, "Don't shoot! I'm harmless!" Tom could not remember the last time he had seen a gun, and was sure he had never seen one from this daunting angle. He added, "I'm lost! Peter Gardener sent me here!"

The mention of Peter Gardener seemed to calm the boy. He lowered the revolver towards the ground, then looked quizzically at Tom and said, raising an eyebrow, "Peter Gardener, you say?"

Tom nodded, relieved, "Peter Gardener, from just up the road, sent me down here."

Ronny studied Tom for a few moments. Ronny's appearance was comical: his messy black hair stuck out in tufts in all directions, and his clothes (a heavy plaid shirt and old jeans) were much too big for him. He wore spectacles, also too big, and, judging by how his eyes never seemed to focus on Tom but rather on a point just behind, or inside Tom, their lenses seemed to be of the wrong prescription. His lips toiled against each other tirelessly, the tongue at times peeking through and hastily retreating, as though he was exerting himself in extremely deep thought. Although he was endearing and even interesting, it was altogether difficult to take the boy seriously. Finally, after a long, tense moment during which Ronny studied Tom from head to foot many times over, Ronny finally said, "Is that so?" but this was clearly not a question.

They all began taking their ease once it seemed that Ronny, who was apparently the leader of sorts, had decided that Tom was no threat. The other boy seemed to be about on the threshold of manhood, about six feet tall and athletically built. He wore a rather simple expression of puzzlement and seemed inherently good-natured. He had short blonde hair which shone healthily in the sun, and his face was fresh and full; he wore a simple white T-shirt with a faded, unidentifiable picture on it, and faded blue jeans. Calpurnia was much younger, still a child. She had reddish hair which was tied back into a ponytail, and she wore a yellow shirt that danced brightly beneath overalls which were too large for her and accumulated at her feet. The other girl seemed to be about the older boy's age, but she was very dirty and shabbily dressed as though she had been living in the woods for some considerable time: her hair and face were dirty, muddying her features, and her clothes were tattered revealing scratched, dirty skin bronzed by the sun.

"Well, if what you say is true," said Ronny, "and I see no reason why it shouldn't be," – he shot a quick interrogative glance at Tom, as to assess the trustworthiness of his face – "then we have strict instructions to bring you to Mother. I am Ronny; this is George; and this is Calpurnia." He gestured at the other two with whom he had been conversing; then, looking at the older, disheveled girl, he added, "She is having problems right now. We just stumbled across her here. She was crying. I don't think she speaks English. I don't know if we'll be able to keep her." He sounded somewhat wistful.

Tom, not displeased, was nonetheless confused. He said, "I am Tom."

"However," Ronny said sharply, his eyes lighting up behind his large spectacles, "we can't keep you unless you have some use. What do you do?"

Tom had not been asked this recently; indeed, he did not think that he had ever been asked the question at all before. But since it seemed important to Ronny that he be able do something, he answered quickly, "Forager," since he had a distinct feeling that he had once been in charge of finding and collecting things, important things, for an important cause. This answer, however, caused Ronny to squint disapprovingly, so Tom quickly corrected himself, "Hunting, er ... and fishing, and I'm a builder. Exploring, too, I do very well ... or so I've been told," he lied, but he felt sure that he was a superb explorer.

This seemed to give Ronny some reassurance; he said, "All right. We'll head back to the house now. Mother will be very glad to see you. She had been told – Father told her – that Peter Gardener would send us someone very important around now ... unless there is some mistake ..." – he looked searchingly at Tom – "I think you are expected."

This last statement was rather surprising to Tom. He was not accustomed, as far as he knew, to being expected, or accounted for, or accommodated. He found it somewhat surreal and even a little unsettling. He wanted to ask more about his being "expected" by Mother, but he thought it wise to hold his tongue and not test the goodwill of his newly acquired company. They began making their way back to the road through the pines through which Tom had just penetrated, and then began going down in the direction of the bay in militant silence. The revolver had disappeared into a small duffel bag carried by George, which seemed to contain other items.

After walking a little way in silence, Ronny fell into step with Tom and began talking. "You see, we are a very strict community – strict obedience to our rules, as set out by Father and his forebears, are what has preserved us for this long. He learned them from his forebears, and they learned it from theirs," – he made expansive gestures with his hands – "and they learned it from the great HP."

Tom, thinking perhaps that he had misheard, queried, "HP?"

Ronny, looking somewhat pleased with himself, said, "Don't tell me you've never heard of HP."

Tom began to feel unsettled again. Something about the initials made him feel uneasy; the letters hung menacingly in the cobbles, empty symbols, casting malignant shadows in their arbitrariness. "No, Ronny," he gulped, "I've never heard of HP."

"Well," beamed Ronny proudly, "That, my friend, is your problem."

Tom suddenly felt very relieved at this easy diagnosis, "I have been feeling quite confused lately."

"And no wonder! Living in aporia all your life! Can you even tell me where you were born? What time it is? Where are you now? Peter Gardener – I've never met the man – must work for a relic of the Dark Ages." He stroked his smooth chin. "Yes, a relic of the Dark Ages indeed."

Tom, reflecting anew upon his circumstances, was bound to admit to himself that he was very confused and wasn't able to answer any of those questions Ronny had just posed. Indeed, he was probably unable to answer any questions at all. Although he had a strange sense of familiarity, even deja-vu, he felt as if he was unable to access a significant portion of his intellect. And how, Tom wondered, did Ronny know where he had lived his whole life? "This HP must be quite a wonder. Will he be able to help me?"

"Oh, he will help you all right," Ronny nodded eagerly, smiling, "He will sort you out."

"I would appreciate it very much. Are we going to see him now?"

Ronny, suddenly serious again, said, "Well, you can't meet him, per se ..." he paused, carefully constructing his next sentence, "You can more than benefit from his powers, as it were;" – he suddenly straightened his spine, and dropped his voice as low as it would go in an effort to achieve a tone of serious importance, the effect of which was somewhat ludicrous – "you can, through careful study, improve yourself, with the help of those of us who have had time with HP." – Tom nodded, interested – "You see, HP's time is running low, alas. He sleeps unless he is absolutely, urgently needed. He has only eleven minutes and forty-six point three two seconds left on his battery! The anxiety, the panic, the horror that this fills us with, has filled our forefathers with, I can not hope to describe to you. In fact, Tom," Ronny looked somewhat downcast, "I myself have only had twenty-one seconds with him. I watched him bestow some vital knowledge upon Father once, and ... I feel very fortunate to have done so. Most people do not get to see HP – he is locked away in the house. Even Father has only had twelve minutes and thirty two seconds with him, making an average of about one point one minute per ten years of his life – Father is one hundred and thirteen ..." Ronny trailed off, thinking about numbers; then, suddenly reanimated, he added, "That is the kind of thing HP could tell us, right down to the very last decimal point, but of course we would never waste his time with such trifles. He is our treasure, our God, really ... indeed, we would never even know about or be able to question the notion of God were it not for HP and the tireless work of our forefathers, who used HP's dwindling minutes to copy down sedulously the tomes of ancient lore – for the immeasurable benefit of our people – until the point was reached where it was decided that the last hour of HP's time must be saved for only the most dire urgencies. And as time passed, naturally, the criteria of urgency became narrower and narrower. And to think of all the time that was wasted on questionable pieces of information ... it never ceases to nag at me ..." Ronny trailed off again, pinching his smooth chin between the pointer and middle fingers of his right hand and shaking his head in disapproval. "You know, life is too short for Schopenhauer." Tom wasn't sure who Schopenhauer was. "If they had spent that time copying something better ... but on one point we are agreed: the musical scores. They have enriched our people to no end." Then, as if suddenly snapping out of a revery, he looked apologetically at Tom, "You must forgive me. Enough about HP. We don't even know if we are supposed to keep you, or send you away, or what."

"Or shoot you!" Calpurnia suddenly interjected. Tom, though quite certain that the little girl was joking, felt a little put off by this remark; but he was put back at ease when all three of them (the disheveled girl was not engaged in the happenings, but was being supported by a concerned-looking George and staring listlessly at her feet) burst into laughter.

"You must ignore Calpurnia. She has a strange sense of humour," said Ronny, chuckling.

The road was straightening out, and the trees were becoming sparser and letting more light onto the ground. Tom could now again see parts of the mountain-cut horizon through gaps in the trees, and he could tell that they were a good bit lower in altitude and probably almost at sea-level. Soon the road ran into another, larger road, over which it appeared more vehicles had passed, for the cobbles were more worn. Tom was a little surprised to see a Georgian carriage to the front of which were harnessed two large, healthy-looking horses. They approached the carriage, then Ronny turned to Tom and said, "I wouldn't expect you to remember this from anything, familiar as I am with the limited extent of your knowledge, but this kind of thing happens all the time in spy stories and things like that: we need to blindfold you before we take you any further. Don't be nervous – it is just for safety. Rules, as I told you, are what have kept our society together all these generations! We have to blindfold both of you," he said, turning to the other girl whom George was in the process of putting into the carriage. Whereupon he walked to the duffel bag which George had left on the cobbles and pulled out a blindfold and proceeded to go behind Tom and tie the blindfold snugly around his eyesockets. The blindfold did not seem too dirty. He led Tom to the carriage, into which Tom was able to climb with minimal difficulty. Tom then felt the carriage crouch under the added weight of Ronny climbing up into the driver's seat atop the carriage, followed by the greater weight of George climbing in through the opposite door, followed by the smallest weight of Calpurnia climbing into the seat across from him. The horses took off at once, though Tom did not hear a command, verbal or otherwise, issued.

They went uphill for a while at a steeper incline than that at which they had just been descending by foot. Tom did not bother to estimate the distance they traveled, but instead occupied himself with wondering as to the properties and qualities of HP: what class of thing was this HP? He wondered the same about Mother: would she be kind and benevolent, or hostile? Deciding that such guesswork was an enterprise of limited potential, Tom's thoughts roamed back again to the dwarf about whom Peter Gardener had warned him. Maybe these seemingly wellmeaning youths would know something about the dwarf and how best not to run into him. Tom eventually decided to ask them about the dwarf, but at a later occasion when perhaps he could speak to Ronny alone. It was wise, he thought, to say something, which may go amiss publicly, in private.

Time passed in silence, the four of them sitting side by side and toe to toe and occasionally bumping into each other when the carriage bounced over an odd uneven cobble; the incline became gradually ever steeper, and Tom felt his ears pop in token that a significantly higher altitude had been reached. Then the slope began to flatten again and the horses began to speed up, causing Tom to infer that they had reached a kind of plateau, and the road seemed to change from cobble to smooth cement. A few minutes later he thought he heard voices and other noises outside the carriage as if they were in a town or something, causing him to hope that they were approaching their destination, for he was wearying of the blindfold and finding it increasingly agitating and unpleasant being taken so far without seeing where he was going.

"Are we almost there?" Tom asked, as cheerily as he could.

"Almost there," said George's voice to the right of him.

They were not close enough for Tom, though. After another couple minutes of waiting in the darkness of the blindfold, in the greater darkness of the silent carriage, in the even greater darkness of the unknown world outside, Tom began to become extremely impatient and restless. His breathing became heavier, and he shifted positions constantly in physical objection.

"Are you all right, Tom?" Calpurnia asked across from him, simultaneously dealing him a sharp kick in his left shin.

"I fear that I am finding this voyage increasingly uncomfortable. Perhaps I could get out to stretch my legs for a while?" Tom responded, trying to restrain his increasingly violent discomfort.

He heard a window slide to the right of him, letting in a sudden gush of noise, of people laughing, talking, arguing in unknown languages, what sounded like a train whistle piercing shrilly over everything, and Tom thought also that he could hear the hissing crash of waves assailing stone walls or cliffs. Some of the voices he thought were oddly familiar, among them George's, obligingly, urgently asking Ronny to stop the carriage and let Tom stretch his legs. The carriage did not stop, however, but rather sped up and started bouncing and skipping violently as if they were riding over broken concrete. The noises became louder, and Tom thought he heard Ronny cry, "I can't stop them!" but he was not sure, for he heard so many other noises and voices, as of many animal and human tongues, that the whole thing became a horrible cacophony of overwhelming, all-too-real sound, rushing right through Tom's eardrums like a hungry, bloodthirsty horde to pour unstoppably into Tom's very mind. Calpurnia screamed; George emitted a low groan of uncertainty; the girl to the right of Tom grabbed his leg and began to wail; Tom covered his ears with his hands and clenched his teeth, rocking himself back and forth convulsively as the carriage threw his body in every other direction. The many noises coalesced to become one horrible monstrous roar, like a gargantuan explosion, an atomic bomb.

Tom was not sure what happened next. His entire perception had been utterly overwhelmed and bombarded far beyond the point of manageability – but, since it was apparently not yet his time to die, or because the perceptual cataclysm was not quite enough to kill him, he simply endured, screaming and convulsing, every bit of his body tense and jittering, as the sounds poured in through the window and the damned stallions of hell dragged the atrocious vehicle over the razor-waves of an infernal stormstricken sea-route, every bump a tsunami, twenty tsunamis per second. Tom could hear only a horrible, ten-times-deafening roar, clouding with blackness his mind's sky.

- 4 -
The House in the Town

Eventually, a soft, gentle hand began to pry Tom's right hand from his right ear; it was a soft but insistent touch, patient and considerate yet determined to pry. The noises were no longer there, but Tom thought he could hear the echo of the roar in his skull. He let his hands down, and heard the door to his left open. The disheveled girl sitting to the right of Tom, her shaky hand still clutched, iron-tight, on his leg, had temporarily stopped weeping and seemed to be catching her breath; Tom took a hold of her wrist and pulled gently until she let go of his leg, hearing her sigh heavily.

Suddenly Tom heard Ronny leap down from atop the carriage and come next to him, saying, "I'm terribly sorry about that, Tom; that was an earthquake. They happen about once a week or so. We are on a fault-line, you see. Anyway, if you want the details I can explain more later, but it would be rather unexciting compared to what we just experienced."

"Have we arrived yet?" asked Tom hopefully, still feeling extremely disoriented.

"No, but you can get out and stretch your legs if you want."

Tom, disappointed, allowed himself to be helped out of the carriage by Ronny and stood on the ground. The road seemed to be as smooth as ever, and Tom decided that it must have been a very strong earthquake to have caused all that shaking, and they must be very close to the so-called "fault-line." Tom thought that they must be at a very high altitude, for the air seemed thinner and it was very windy; he had not felt the carriage go downhill after all that climbing, unless that had happened during the earthquake. Tom stretched, trying to relish his freedom from the cramped, oppressive carriageride. However, eager to get to their destination and be done with the blindfold, Tom declared that he was ready to go on and was led back to the door of the carriage by Ronny.

In a moment they were off again. The ride was smooth once more, and Tom felt a merciful kind of pleasant fuzz descend upon his tired nerves, possibly some aftereffect of the trauma of the earthquake and the accompanying skull-splitting noise. He felt as though a part of himself, his body or his mind or some vital part in which both were fused inseparably, was resting, sleeping even, after having been pushed exhaustingly beyond a verge never before crossed; he himself was not sleeping, but he felt as though some small but important part had been given ten minutes' much-needed leave in order to recollect itself. He sat back idly like a mother watching her child sleep after a long tiring tantrum. The carriage began to go downhill, at an agreeably gentle pace. Gravity sucked his limbs into the floor and the leather seat, and his body bounced like a buoy on a calm lake's waves. Every once in a while, however, he thought he felt a nearly imperceptible shudder reverberate from the ground up through the wheels, but this was so slight that it was easy to ignore, or to fail to notice entirely, or to tell himself that he was simply imagining it.

After some time had passed the carriage came to a slow stop. Tom, no longer in any hurry to leave the carriage or shed his blindfold but rather still engulfed in the calming fuzz, remained slouched in the leather seat until he felt a small hand undo the blindfold from the back of his head. After his eyes had adjusted to their newfound freedom, Tom was welcomed by an amused-looking Calpurnia sitting directly opposite him, to the right of whom a sympathetic-looking George was seated contemplating how best to wake the disheveled girl who was seated next to Tom and whose hand was, oddly, once again clutched no less tightly above his right knee. Tom, feeling awkward, grabbed her wrist and pulled gently but forcefully until her hand reluctantly relinquished his leg, but she did not wake. Her breathing was peaceful, and it was perhaps this appearance of happy sleep that made George decide to leave her as she was, lest upon waking she begin to cry again, or worse. They clambered out of the carriage, Tom feeling especially weak after the paralyzing comfort of the descent.

After stretching and apologizing to his amusedly forgiving companions, Tom took a look at his surroundings, and was somewhat surprised by what he saw. They were in the gravel parking lot of a two-story house with a wide porch and with a balcony perched above, on a road along which were evenly arrayed other similarly sized but differently styled houses (in a word, suburbia, but Tom did not think of this word). However, the houses all appeared to be abandoned; there were about a half-dozen people of both genders scattered here and there, but they were on the front yard of the house in whose driveway the carriage was parked, staring at Tom with various shades of curiosity, sympathy, fear, and hostility as they engaged in activities which Tom did not understand involving objects which Tom did not recognize, thus giving the impression that this house was the only house on the street that was occupied. Upon closer inspection, it appeared that many of the other houses on the street were missing siding, and one could see into rooms in some of the houses because so much of their walls had been taken apart or collapsed. Aside from these aspects of dilapidation, the yards of all the houses were grown into hayfields; there were a few automobiles in some of the driveways but they were all rusted to a dark brown and many without tires; and what few telephone poles stood suspended no wires and it appeared that some of the poles had been chopped down with an axe. Tom found it all very unusual; he had a strong feeling that places like these should not be like this. As far as he could make out, the house before which they were gathered was the only intact one, except for a redbrick one which appeared to be undamaged, up the road at the corner where an adjoining street ran into theirs from the left, the roadsign at the corner of which Tom could barely read as naming their road Warren and the other Meade.

Ronny left the company to go up the porch and inside the house, and Tom stood staring at the no longer neighbourhood, trying to make sense of what he saw. Tom had many questions. Indeed, he had so many that he was unable to order them properly in his mind, so he decided not to ask any of them but rather to let things happen of their own accord. Things have gone well enough so far, he said to himself, although in truth he was somewhat perturbed, retrospectively, by the fact that he could feel as intensely horrible as he did some moments during the recent carriageride without passing out or dying. The pleasant fuzzy revery which had descended upon him shortly thereafter was hardly worth the shock of the peculiar sensory onslaught – the so-called "earthquake." It was possible, he considered, that, conversely, now that he had experienced such extreme unpleasantness he was unlikely to experience something equally awful, or was that just wishful thinking? He wondered if the dwarf about whom Peter had warned him was capable of inflicting something comparably unpleasant upon his person, or perhaps the dwarf would kill him? Torture him, perhaps, in some surprising and novel way? There are some things worse than death, Tom considered, probably a good many things. This led him to wonder if he would have preferred death to his recent earthquake experience, and the answer was clearly no, it was not worth dying in order to avoid. Prolonged to any extent, it would certainly have been intolerable, and death would have been infinitely preferable. God forbid it ever last an eternity. That, Tom thought, would have been hell.

Suddenly Ronny was at Tom's shoulder, saying, "Mother will see you now. Follow me, please."

Ronny led the way towards the small side-staircase of the porch; Calpurnia said bye and disappeared, and George stayed waiting by the carriage. The people in the yard had lost interest in Tom, and a couple of them, young fellows in jeans and shortsleeved shirts, came and began talking to George regarding the girl in the carriage. Tom heard George explain that she was in bad shape.

Tom and Ronny walked onto the porch, the white paint of which was almost completely peeled off, and up to the front door. Ronny paused for a moment and looked up at Tom in his somewhat ludicrously yet quite endearingly earnest way and said, "No-one is allowed inside the house without special permission from Mother. Most of the rooms are locked, anyway. Rules, you see." With a key he opened the front door, and they entered a small whitepainted vestibule which led to two doorways on the first story and a staircase leading to the second. There was a coat-rack which bore many hats and coats of different varieties, and miscellaneous things lay piled up in the corners of the room: shoes, boots, ropes, metal objects which Tom did not immediately recognize, tent-pegs, canvases, walking-sticks, an axe and hatchets, shovels, and other things.

"The place is filled with junk, mostly," Ronny explained, "but there are also some extremely valuable things which we simply cannot do without." He smiled, "Mother, for instance, and Father, and HP. And our books, and the musical instruments, and other things ..."

He led the way up the stairs into a hallway which was painted with the same bleak white as the vestibule. There were dirt-marks on the walls where shoulders had rubbed, seemingly over many years, and there were stains on the ceiling where water had leaked. There was a long bookcase running along the length of the hallway which reached to the ceiling and which contained not books but papers stacked in various ways. There were five rooms, the doors to which were all shut, in the hallway: three were located directly at the top of the stairs and the other two at the end of the hallway which ran back along the length of the staircase to meet the wall above the front door where another sixth door opened out onto the balcony, through the window of which the sun, now higher in the sky, threw its beams in a swathe on the wall above the staircase, to the right and left of which door the other doors were located.

The fifth room, to the right of the balcony door, was the one to which Ronny led Tom. He put an attentive ear to the door, knocked lightly thrice, then pushed it open. The room was dark, the blinds drawn over the two windows letting in only a faint glow of light. The room was not heavily furnished: there was a dressing table with a mirror against the far wall; a bed against the wall to the right of the doorway; a chest of drawers against the doorway's wall; another bookcase against the wall to the left of the doorway, again filled with papers but also with a few books here and there; and in the middle of the room sat an old armchair, draped with blankets, upon which sat a lady whose features were hard to distinguish because of the darkness.

"Here he is, Mother," said Ronny softly.

"Throw open the blinds, boy, I want to get a good look at him," she said briskly, her voice rather unexpectedly high-pitched.

Ronny went over to each window and threw open the blinds. Mother, whom the daylight revealed to be younger than Tom had expected and quite goodlooking with light brown hair, full breasts and wide hips beneath a blue flowery dress, smiled apologetically at Tom, saying, "You must forgive the darkness. I have a headache." Her gaze, playful, had a somewhat dizzying effect on Tom.

Once Ronny had finished opening the blinds, he came back to stand before Mother, his head bowed deferentially. She looked at him lovingly, concernedly, and said, "Where did you find him?"

"Near the bay, down the road from the castle. He was alone. We had just found the other one, and then he showed up."

Mother looked at Tom thoughtfully, the pointer finger of her right hand tapping on the arm of the chair. Nodding, she asked, "Tom?"

Tom nodded and answered, "Peter Gardener sent me."

She smiled at him approvingly, then her eyes darted up at the ceiling as if she had just remembered something important. She said, "Yes, Father told me something about you ..." – she knit her eyebrows in token of vexation – "but I'll be darned if I can remember what it was right now." She flinched in mock frustration, then said to Tom, "I'll go see if he can remember."

She rose nimbly from her seat and walked swiftly past Tom and out the door, covering him with a cloud of sweet flowery aroma. Tom found her very attractive, and he looked at Ronny with an embarrassed apologetic glance. Ronny, however, was looking at the floor in apparent consternation and said nothing. They stood in silence until she returned. "No," she said, "Father is sleeping right now and he so hates it when I wake him up." She smiled pleasantly, "Why don't I show you around the house?"

Ronny looked up quickly and said urgently, "There's another one, Mother; remember that other one I told you about?"

"Other one?" she asked, then pouted and said, disappointedly, "I guess you should take your friend ... what was your name?" she looked at Tom questioningly, the wet orbs of her eyes gleaming.

"Tom," answered Ronny.

"Yes," she said, "take Tom out for a hunt." She looked at Tom, blinking in flirtatious fashion, and said, "Why don't you lovely boys go out and catch us a rabbit, or a duck, or ..." – she rolled her eyes along the ceiling hungrily – "a bear. I'll talk to you later, Tom," she said, giving Tom a last stupefying smile.

Ronny led the way out of the room, and Tom followed, somewhat downcast, for he had quickly become fond of the lady's alluring presence. Ronny, however, rather than taking Tom outside as Mother had instructed, after closing the door to Mother's room led the way to the door directly across therefrom, on the other side of the balcony door, and whispered, "She won't mind if I show you something. I promise you have never seen anything like it. This is the only one I've ever heard of, at least. But don't say a word and tread softly; Father is sleeping." He pulled out his keychain, inserted a key into the doorknob, and gently pushed the door open. The room was very bright: both windows were open, letting in great splashes of sunlight onto the floor and onto the wall through which they had entered. Tom noticed that the room was nearly completely unfurnished: there was only a desk against the far wall before which sat a very old and tattered swivel chair, and nothing else. Tom, expecting the never-before-seen, was, needless to say, unimpressed. He looked at Ronny with spread eyebrows in anticipation of further revelation.

Ronny looked at Tom amusedly, slightly mischievously in his endearingly precocious manner, and whispered, "It gets better, sir." He strolled over to the desk and began looking like he was possibly preparing to open one of the four drawers stacked along the left of the leg-space beneath the desktop. Then he stopped and whispered, "I'd better check if maybe he is awake. Stay where you are." He walked lightly over to a closet door in the wall to the left and very slowly pulled it open. He looked over to Tom and gestured with his forefinger for him to come nearer. Tom did, and when he came near enough to see into the closet he got a tremendous shock.

The closet was of medium size, into which one could walk but not too far. There was nothing in the closet except for one thing (or assembly of things) which in its strangeness and apparent complexity more than made up for the barrenness of the room. What Tom saw, in chronological order, was a copper-coloured cylindrical metallic barrel-like thing, about three feet across and four feet tall, from which sprang many tubes and wires and upon which were arrayed many knobs and switches and buttons and blinking lights and trembling dials and ticking clocks, and which emitted a low humming noise which was not loud enough for Tom to have heard before the closet door was opened; a plethora of gadgets of various description which Tom didn't recognize were strewn at the foot of the barrel, to some of which were attached many of the aforementioned tubes and wires; and atop this pile of machinery was affixed the most incredible thing, the sight of which made Tom's heart skip a beat in abject horror: a transparent cylindrical jar-like object, about a foot wide and two feet tall, filled to capacity by a pale green bubbling fluid in which bobbled a bald wrinkled male human head whose eyeballs fluttered behind closed lids in the twitches of REM sleep. The face wore a satisfied smile.

"That's Father," whispered Ronny to Tom, "Handsome, isn't he?" Then he quietly closed the door before continuing, "Usually we don't bring anybody in here, except in rare circumstances."

Tom felt nauseated by the sight by which he had just been confronted; certainly he had not expected to see anything like that. He was completely uninterested in Ronny's last statement, although part of his reeling mind wished that Ronny had not made an exception to the rule by letting him in here but had rather withheld this closeted marvel. Tom felt weak in his legs and wanted to sit down.

Ronny, seeing that Tom was flustered by his introduction to Father, said simply, "Yes, not everybody has a relative who has been thus immortalized." Then, heedless of Tom's distress, he tiptoed over to the desk and with another key opened the top drawer. He looked at Tom with a proud smile, which, excessive and caricature-like, inflected sickeningly Tom's nausea and increased it, and gestured again for Tom to approach, saying, "And now, the wonder of the known world!"

Tom approached unsteadily, wanting only get out of the room, to vomit and lie down in the hayfield outside; he was sweating heavily, and felt very warm and dizzy. In the drawer sat a very low, flat, thin, wide rectangular grey case-like object, sparklingly clean, in the center of which were engraved, upside down, the initials HP. Tom, not understanding, not caring, thinking it was all some kind of joke, retreated from the room and from Ronny's smile, the lips around which were whispering, "The gift of the ages, the wisdom of our forefathers, Tom, the very zenith of human accomplishment!"

Tom fled down the stairs as quietly as he could lest he should arouse a fracas, then out through the vestibule onto the front porch. Ronny was quick to follow him, but Tom was not aware of that, overwhelmed as he was by the closet's surprise. The predictable questions of pragmatic nature were far from his thoughts as he stumbled to the edge of the porch and let loose an outpouring of puke onto the overgrown front yard, to the mixed reactions of amusement, bemusement, and surprise of the onlookers. The vision of Father's head, wrinkled and bald in the pale green fluid, hovered in the backdrop of Tom's mind as he shuddered in a heap on the porch railing, ridding himself of unidentifiable stuff. Father's fluttering eyes played Tom's quivering body like puppeteers: Father's fluttering eyes as he dreamed in his fluid, crossing plains, trekking forests, reaching places, oases perhaps, drinking of the waters and moving onwards, on to mountains, valleys, oceans and cities, castles and lakes, obtaining enormous riches: dreams ever beautiful in content, his smile of satisfied contentment branding its deep permanent mark into Tom's imagination.

- 5 -
The Hunt by the River

After Tom's bout of vomiting was done with, he became aware that a good many people were laughing at him, some hysterically. There were some noises of sympathy, some of disgust, but the overall theme of the noises was overwhelmingly one of laughter. Tom, very embarrassed and still rather shaken, did not find it funny, although he was relieved that no-one appeared to be angry at him. Ronny was at his elbow, and he put his hand on Tom's back which was still hunched over the porch railing. Tom's vision was spinning, but it was a fun, happy spinning, one of grateful riddance. He was drenched in sweat which was now cooling pleasantly. He did not feel bad anymore, just shaken.

"I must say," said Ronny, "that Father tends to have that effect on people, even those who are accustomed to seeing preserved personalities! Father never had a particularly ... easy personality, I mean." Ronny laughed, "Take your time! I have things to do."

Ronny left, and Tom slowly raised himself up from the railing, leaned up against a porch pillar, and looked about him, feeling very ashamed and upset for having vomited before so many strangers. There were about ten people gathered in the yard now, some engaged in activities which Tom did not understand in a polite effort to ignore him; others, less considerate, leered and laughed at him.

"Sorry about that," Tom said, then walked towards the centre porch stairs, which were wide, with the intention of sitting upon them and deciding what to do next. His earlier attitude of curiosity and interest in the situation had vanished, and he was now purposed to reassess the situation, so far as this was possible. He was possessed at that moment by an overpowering feeling of senselessness, of primal confusion, which was also actually quite invigorating as it wiped away the muddled surface of superficial concerns and confronted him with the vital core of his incomprehension. He no longer felt bad physically, but he had no idea what he should do with himself; he knew only that he was alive, and had an empty stomach, and there was an odd kind of exuberance in that. He sat on the third step, resting his elbows upon his knees and folding his hands together, staring at the gravel path which led to the stairs and beginning to wonder what, if anything, would fill his stomach again – had not there been talk of bears? He wondered what bear tasted like, but hoped that someone else would do the killing of it. Hardly a moment had passed before he perceived a small person sitting to his right.

"I'm going to start reading Plato tomorrow," Calpurnia's voice chirped. "But I don't want to."

Tom, grateful for the introduction of a new and random subject yet entirely ignorant of Plato, suggested, "Then don't."

"But I have to!"

"Oh," Tom said, "I see." There was a silence as Tom thought of something to say; then he said, "Well, Calpurnia, darling, it seems to me that, if the situation is as you describe, then sometimes one must do things one doesn't want to do." The sentence was formed and uttered without any volition on Tom's part.

"But I don't want to!"

"Hmm," said Tom. "Perhaps you don't give Plato enough credit. Perhaps you have got him the wrong way. Maybe, just perhaps, you will even like Plato and meet him one day when you grow up, and marry him."

"Ew! That's gross!" She dealt him a sharp kick just above his right ankle, causing him to cry out in pain.

"Sorry," said Tom, reflecting that perhaps his comment had been a bad one, not least because Plato was probably dead, going by

Ronny's statements as to the antiquity of their reading material. "Why don't you want to read Plato?"

But he did not get to hear the answer because Ronny jumped down the steps swiftly and stood before the two, and said, "Want to go for a hunt? You must be hungry after discarding your supplies like that."

"Oooh! Can I come too?" cried Calpurnia.

Ronny chuckled as though he had expected her to say that, and said, "I suppose, but you know the rules: do everything I tell you to do and shut up when I tell you to."

Ronny began walking back towards the carriage, and Tom and Calpurnia followed him. The carriage was empty, the doors shut, and Tom presumed that the disheveled girl had been taken upstairs to see Mother; George also was missing. Ronny stood next to the carriage for a moment and looked around searchingly. After a few seconds he shrugged and jumped up onto the driving seat of the carriage, then nodded at Tom and Calpurnia that they should follow him. Tom and Calpurnia each climbed up the side of the carriage and sat on either side of Ronny: Calpurnia to his left and Tom to his right. The three of them filled the seat. Ronny gave a sharp, soundless snap of the reins and the horses lurched into motion, steadily and dutifully. The one on the right was a shiny black horse; the one on the left was white and brown. They were both very large and muscular, and performed their schlepping with paramilitant gusto, the observance of which caused Tom to reflect that despite a certain indefinable roughness about the edges, the group in whose clutches he currently found himself seemed to have all of their important machinery in fine working order.

Tom was curious as to what Mother had forgotten, and did not appreciate the deferral of a revelation he had been awaiting with some anxiety. Mother was an eager, generous host, and a very attractive lady, he reflected, but was she perhaps a little senile? One must not be fooled by appearances, he told himself. Given what he had seen in the closet, it was very possible that Mother was in fact a very old lady. Ronny had told Tom that his father was no less than one hundred and thirteen years old. In short, Tom was prepared to believe anything now. Clearly he was in some sort of miraculous magical world in which anything was possible. Suffice it to say his speculations at this time were of a wild and farflung nature.

One speculation, however, Tom avoided for now, and this was the question of the mechanics of procreation in the strange family he had just met. He avoided this partly because to think about it still made him feel queazy, the possibilities being potentially too monstrous, and partly because now that he was more or less acquainted with and accepted by Ronny he felt that to think about such things was in poor taste. But of course, Ronny's mother was very attractive, never mind the shortcomings of her partner parent, and the question still nagged at the back of his mind, as one would expect it to.

The voyage on top of the carriage, unblindfolded, was a great improvement over his previous confinement in the passenger booth. As the horses picked up speed, the wind crept up his back and sides and made the sweat chill him refreshingly and made his shirt stick to his back frigidly. They rode up the road through the post-suburbia, which was of the older type characterized by every house being in some way unique (as opposed to mass-produced lookalikes). But the houses all appeared to be abandoned; the grass grew long in every yard; vines climbed up walls and swallowed some houses whole; great gashes opened walls exposing rotted wood, fungi, soggy brown furniture; rusted cars sat sadly in their driveways like dry crumpled insects; large trees were fallen into weak papery roofs like broadswords chopped into helmets. The noise of the wind, for it was a windy morning, together with the creak and clatter of the wheels on the cracked pavement were not conducive to conversation, so the carriageride went on without talk.

If it had been nighttime, the neighbourhoods would doubtless have been eerie in their long-neglected ghostliness, but as it was morning Tom felt excited and adventurous. Furthermore, there was something imposingly and portentously awe-inspiring about the carriageride. Even though all evidence pointed to something tremendous having already happened and passed away long ago, the neighbourhoods, the town, everything seemed to promise that something even larger, more awesome, something absolutely stupendous was right now in the process of beginning to happen, to which the previous tremendous thing was but prologue. This feeling was an abstract one, without specificity, but it caused him to feel another, more specific feeling, namely, that his time here, in this place with these people, was somehow stolen away and he had been given leave to do wild, mad, and unimagined things. He felt that if the world of responsibility existed, it existed far away beyond the horizon, or it had perished long ago and now lay still beneath layers of vines and fungi like the houses of the town. He felt adventurous and free, even aggressive in his will to express and explore to its full extent the powerful sensation in his breast.

They turned a few corners, passed a few open spaces which appeared to have once been parks, and then they started going downhill at a gradual incline, and Tom could get a clear view of part of the surrounding countryside which had hitherto been hidden by the houses and tall trees of the curving blocks of the post-suburbia. They appeared to be in a small valley, and it looked like they were headed down towards the valley's river. On the other side of the supposed river was some farmland – fields, farmhouses, barns and silos – and a highway heading off into the horizon cleft the cool greenery of the woods and fields. There appeared to be a rather elegant redbrick building set amid the forest far in the distance. (Because of the height of the buildings and trees on either side of the road, Tom's long-distance vision was confined to what was ahead beyond the road down which they were heading.) The sun was now higher in the sky: it appeared to be the middle of the morning. The cumulus clouds, harmless as ever, occasionally covered the sun, and it was quite windy, but it was a warm wind and overall the weather was very agreeable. The valley was overwhelmingly beautiful, the sky crisp and the sun infinitely benevolent. The whole valley and sky bespoke endless promise and fulfillment, bringing to Tom's mind some of the last words Peter Gardener had spoken to him: "The world will be beautiful no matter what kinds of stories we manage to tell ourselves." At this moment, clopping down the main road of the abandoned town, Tom felt strongly the rightness of these words, and also felt grateful that Peter had shared them with him.

There were larger buildings now, all abandoned and dilapidated in various ways: schools; stores with blank-faced display cases; restaurants with broken windows; a townhall with a collapsed roof; churches with gaping doorways; a post office; a couple gas stations. Tom enjoyed looking at all this for a while, and then they came up to a crossroads (or intersection) where their road crossed what was evidently another main road. Traffic lights hung over the road glaring with vacant black eyes, offering no instruction where none was needed. There was no traffic, but Ronny nonetheless whoahed the horses to a stop and looked both ways down the intersecting road, his eyes narrowed to a squint. Apparently satisfied, he started the horses again with a twitch at the reins down the same road they had been going, towards the supposed river. The town soon opened up: large driveways spread out between the buildings, and then they went through an open area of industrial warehouses. Eventually, passing these, they passed some large redbrick apartment buildings, also apparently abandoned, and then they turned rightwards off the main road, down a little gravel road which took them between two buildings and then over a railroad which, predictably, was in a crooked state of disrepair. The gravel road took them over a small field then, and finally led to the border of a forest into which it dove straight.

Ronny slowed the horses with a subtle word, looked at Tom and said, "Now is the time to prove yourself: show us those hunting skills you talked about."

He stopped the carriage a little way into the forest, then hopped off the carriagetop and helped Calpurnia down, and Tom disembarked by the other side and went around the carriage to meet them, hoping that he was not in over his head: he doubted he would fare well against a bear. He found Ronny searching neck-deep in a compartment on the back of the carriage, with Calpurnia kicking at the gravel at the side of the road and staring off idly into the forest. Ronny emerged a moment later bearing a short glintyheaded spear in his right hand about five feet long, a machete in his left hand, and a young excited grin on his face; he handed the weapons to Tom. Tom, feeling extremely doubtful, took them as confidently as he could; he had told Ronny that he was a hunter, and did not want to disappoint him for fear of the consequences. Ronny then again put his head and arms into the compartment and made noises which sounded like he was searching through a huge assortment of metallic and wooden objects. He reemerged bearing another short spear, another machete, and a small knife. He whistled at Calpurnia, she turned lazily and he threw the knife a few feet before her. She jumped back, Ronny laughed, and she said, after regaining her composure, "You idiot." Ronny laughed again, Calpurnia picked up the knife at her feet, and Ronny went around to the side of the carriage, Tom and Calpurnia behind him, and opened the door to the booth. He pulled out two handguns, to Tom's mixed bemusement (for he was frightened of guns) and relief (for he didn't trust the Dark Age weaponry of spear and blade against the unknown creatures of the world); Ronny handed one to Tom with a serious look which bespoke, "Just in case."

Tom put the gun in his jeans' right forepocket, and without a word Ronny began leading them down a little path which turned off from the road and went downhill through the woods at a gentle angle. Ronny's attitude was unworried, so Tom let his guard down and began to ponder upon his situation as he was becoming accustomed to doing when he had a moment to himself. He hoped his hunting skills would not be tested too much. He was glad that he had a gun in case things got out of hand, but would he really be able to use it effectively if it really came down to it? He was uncertain, careful not to underestimate the difficulties of hunting, and tried to clear his mind and sharpen his perception so as to be at the top of his abilities, which were as yet to him of unknown quality. Part of him felt sure that he could take on anything, but a deeper, perhaps somewhat dormant part soberly told him not to be overconfident.

Tom began making practice swings with the machete in the air, and looked up ahead to make sure that he would not injure Ronny thereby only to discover that Ronny was nowhere in sight. He stopped, bemused that he had lost Ronny so quickly. He then heard the light clapping of Calpurnia's feet as she scampered up behind him; her voice said, "Don't worry: he's just scouting."

"Oh," said Tom, reassured: there didn't seem to be much danger yet.

They walked on a little bit more in silence, Tom gripping his machete appraisingly, trying to get used to its weight distribution. The trees began to thicken around them, and then the path came to a small kind of cliff which jutted out from the trees and gave them a wonderful view of the valley and a beautiful wide river which snaked through it, about two hundred meters down from where they looked, flowing leftwards, northwards according to the sun which was beginning to reach its glorious late-morning zenith. The two stopped for a moment, enjoying the splendid view of the morning's valley. There was no building in sight, no evidence of humanity, although Tom knew that the abandoned town was just a half-kilometer or so behind them, and knew also a bridge probably stretched over this river just around the bend to their far left. Green gushed from everywhere: bright meadows scattered over thick forest of ancient trees opening their branches ecstatically up to heaven, waving in windblown celebration. It was a beautiful place, a marvelous sight, and Tom momentarily forgot his most recent worries of bears. He took in the scene, the endless promise of a springtime morning, the sun reflecting at them from every leaf, every wisp of warmth in the sky above them, and breathed deeply.

After a few moments they continued down the path, which wound around the side of the rock ledge and took them down through the trees towards the river. In a tone more serious and mature than Tom had hitherto heard from her, Calpurnia said, "Some things Father lets us read, and some things he doesn't let us read."

Tom, seeing again the wrinkled head in the green fluid, said, "Is that so?"

"Yes," Calpurnia said decisively, "it is."

"Hmm."

"Ronny is a very busy boy, and everyone around here just minds their own business. Mother ... is forgetful. I have been in the house when everyone was sleeping," she said slyly, "many times, Tom, and taken a look at the books."

"Good stuff?" Tom queried.

"Yes," she inhaled deeply, then said, "Tom, I won't hold back a sigh at this point. There are days when I am haunted by a feeling that is blacker than the blackest melancholy – a contempt for humanity. And just to remove any doubts about what I despise, who I despise: people these days, the people I have been fated to call my contemporaries. People these days – I feel suffocated by their filthy breath ... Like all researchers I have a lot of tolerance for the past, which is to say I exercise generous self-restraint: I go through the madhouse worlds of whole millennia, whether they are called 'Christianity,' 'Christian faith,' or the 'Christian church' with a sort of bleak caution ..." – she paused briefly to catch her breath – "I am careful not to hold humanity responsible for its mental illnesses. But my feelings suddenly change and erupt when I come to more recent times, to our times. Our age knows better ... What used to be just sickness is indecency today ..." – she stopped walking and looked at Tom with wide, earnest eyes – "It is indecent to be a Christian these days."[1]

When Tom was sure she was finished, he said, "Calpurnia, I had no idea you were so ... impassioned ... and complicated ... and tortured!"

"It gets very tough sometimes, Tom."

"What's this, um ... Christianity you're on about?"

"Oh ... it doesn't matter, Tom," she sighed exasperatedly.

"I see. Well, don't let it get to you, Calpurnia; I'm sure one day you'll look back at this period of your life and realize that it was a necessary, albeit difficult phase at the dawn of a marvelous career."

Calpurnia seemed cheered, laughed and said, "Oh Tom, that's nice of you to say, but ... actually I have to confess something."

"What's that? I'm sure it's going to be all right."

"Yes, well, those weren't actually my words, though I treasure them and feel them deep in my heart; they belong to a man, a wonderful man, called Frydish Nitskee."

---

[1] Calpurnia is quoting a passage from Section 38 of Friedrich Nietzsche's *The Anti-Christ.*

"Frydish Nitskee," Tom repeated slowly, stroking his chin. Tom had never heard of Frydish Nitskee, but he had a strong name and sounded very important. Certainly his words were very impressive.

"He's such a beautiful man! An endlessly complex suffering genius! An artist hero! I want to marry him when I grow up. I love him!" She jumped up exuberantly, and cried up into the trees, causing some birds to take off in fright: "I love Nitskeeeee!"

Tom thought it best not to point out that Nitskee was probably dead long ago, preferring to let her realize this in time, when she would be better able to handle it. Of course, Tom thought, remembering Father, it was always possible that this character was preserved somewhere in like state, but that was hardly any consolation. Tom imagined a chamber somewhere filled with preserved personalities, sleeping, talking, laughing, debating, cursing each other and having an uproariously great time.

"But I suppose he's already married, such a wonderful man," Calpurnia reflected sorrowfully. "I wonder what he looks like ..." she sighed and looked longingly off into the trees as though in search of her love's face among the brambles and the leaves.

They walked along a bit more in silence, and Tom thought he could hear faintly the sounds of the river, and the air was becoming cooler. Suddenly Ronny was upon them again, coming at them suddenly out of the brambles, excited and breathless. He said, "Come this way."

They followed him through the bracken, through a little ditch, and then up a steep little hill, holding onto branches and bushes for support and choosing their footholds carefully in an effort not to fall down. When they had reached the top of the little hill, they could see down through the trees the glimmer of riverwater.

Ronny, now serious, stopped them and whispered, "I've tracked it up to here. Look: it's injured." He pointed at some blood on the ground. Tom did not ask what "it" was, again wanting not to reveal his lack of hunting experience; instead he nodded seriously. Ronny continued, "Don't use your gun unless you absolutely have to; try to take it down with the spear, then finish it off with the machete. You got it?" – Tom nodded – "Okay: I'll go this way, and you go that way." Ronny pointed down towards the river. "Be careful! Injured bears are angry bears." This last statement shocked Tom, as one would expect: he did not want to encounter this bear, injured or otherwise.

Before Tom could say anything, however, Ronny darted off through the trees, leaving him with Calpurnia. Tom, trying not to let his fear show on his face, clutched his weapons tightly and decided to go slowly down to the river and wait it out as safely as he could. Calpurnia seemed unworried, but she was probably used to being with an experienced hunter, like George perhaps, and thought Tom to be one himself, and was thus possessed by an ignorant sense of security when in fact her young, promising life was very likely right now in great danger of being ended before it had really begun. This added consideration strengthened Tom's resolution to make his way slowly to the riverside as though he knew exactly what he was doing and then, once there, sit by the river and try to make as little noise as possible. As for Calpurnia? It appeared that he would have to make a riverside confession of ineptitude, and, relying on her youthful goodwill and her rebellious intellectual sway, hope her to be considerate and merciful, and keep it to herself afterwards.

Turning to Calpurnia, Tom brought his right forefinger to his lips in token that she should be quiet, then turned again, as stealthily as he could manage, back down towards the river, and crouching began making his way through the bracken to the water which glimmered whitely through the leaves from below. A few moments later they emerged onto a small sand-ledge which rose about four feet above the water before falling steeply into it. The water was calm by the shore but rushed and hissed loudly in the middle of the river. Tom walked to the edge of the ledge and assembled his brow into an expression at once serious, assertive, and apologetic before turning to Calpurnia to make his confession. When he turned to Calpurnia, however, he got a pretty big shock.

No more than fifteen feet behind Calpurnia was sitting, very much like a human would sit, with its back leaned against a tree at the foot of the riverside hill, a huge brown bear which had not yet noticed them, as it appeared to be contemplating and occasionally licking a wound on its paw. Its handsome hairy face wore a very human look of worry, as though it didn't know what it should do with its present dilemma, and hoped it would not lead to further trouble. Thus Tom's eyes never settled on Calpurnia, and his carefully arranged brow began a slow process of creeping up his forehead, gathering wrinkles as it went as a boat's prow raises waves as it cuts through the water.

Time slowed down for Tom considerably at this point. Tom's initial surprise, lasting no more than a second, was followed by a sure realization that he would not react properly to the situation. Calpurnia, seeing Tom's gaze fix over her little shoulder, began to turn around just as the bear looked up, drunkenly and somewhat sheepishly, with an expression very much like a human would have when caught in a compromising situation. The following exchange took place in a couple of seconds, as such exchanges always do: the bear's eyes told Tom that it was helpless at this moment; Tom knew that it would have been the easiest thing to run over to the bear with the spear and stab it forcefully numerous times in the throat, chest and stomach, but he knew also that he would not do this, and his eyes told the bear just that; the bear, acknowledging that Tom was for some reason incapable of killing it as it would be so easy to do, began, lazily and with disappointment at having to get up from its seat, to get up, very much like a drunkard or sleeper who has been roused against his will, and then began shaking its head in an effort to summon strength and resolve and bearlike aggressiveness. By now Calpurnia was turned around and saw the bear, and she began to tell Tom that there was the bear, but time was still going slowly. Tom's eyes were fixed stupidly on the bear's face, which began shaking vigorously: the lips around its fangs flapped loosely about; stray hairs and bits of dust and spittle flew off into the air; its eyes closed in determination, the bear trying to snap into fighting mode. This took a number of seconds, and by then Calpurnia had uttered her superfluous sentence. Tom, now even more transfixed by the bear's face, continued to do nothing. After staring at the bear for a few seconds, during which the bear rolled forward onto its one good forepaw, turned its head up and looked at Tom like a drunken brawler barely able to walk straight, as if to say, "Well, here I come. I gave you a chance; I don't want to maul you; I am hurting here, and tired, but if I must, then here I come," Calpurnia began to run away from them, down the edge of the river (despite the slowness of time, Calpurnia's disappearance seemed not to take much time at all). Then, seeing that Calpurnia had vanished and that Tom was not about to move, the bear, still unwilling to begin the advance, decided that maybe he could get Tom to go away too with a good roar. It began to brace itself for a roar, closing its eyes momentarily like a revered orator about to deliver a brilliant and much-anticipated speech. After giving Tom a little accidental look, like an actor who notices an audience member and thereby momentarily breaks the illusion by inadvertently acknowledging the artifice of his craft, it began, headfirst, to rear its way skyward, like a dolphin jumping out of the water, and halfway to its airy destination it opened its mouth and began to roar.

It seemed, in the performance that followed, to undergo every emotion under the sun of which animal is capable. It was the most eloquent piece of body language Tom had ever seen, by a long shot. It contained, within its wild writhes and expressive mimes and significant gesticulations, every bit of rage, indignation, threatening, warning, vulgarity, greed, hunger, determination, passion, elation, love, timidity, yearning, loss, sorrow, despair, desperation, hopelessness, grief, sickness, exhaustion, resignation, empathy, tension, anxiety, terror, pain, reproof, slovenliness, satisfaction, generosity, relaxation, relief, joy, triumph, hilarity, melancholy, nostalgia, pointlessness, humility, tragedy, nobility of suffering, futility, excess of pride, boredom of pleasure, ugliness of hatred, carelessness of lust, fantasy of youth, horror of death, intensity of life, soreness of arthritis, impossibility of stasis, that was contained within its big bear's soul, and many other more complex emotions made up of various degrees of those simple emotions mixed together in ambiguous emotional offspring, far more horrible and wonderful than their parents had ever imagined they could be, and even more infinitely subtle emotions made up of marriages of these offspring emotions. It seemed to take Tom, in the square three feet of air it took to perform this roar, into every corner of the universe, every galaxy of every colour, every hot planet seared by its wrathful sun, every cold planet exiled far from warmth on its lonely millennium-long orbit, every perilous asteroid belt, every black hole, stopping for a moment at every place to relish the spot in full before moving on. Tom felt as though the journey had taken hours, but in reality the roar had not lasted much longer than a normal roar. It was a magical journey, and undoubtedly the finest performance Tom had ever seen, or, in all likelihood, that he would ever see. The bear even managed, between its myriad expressions, to sneak a few glances at Tom to check his reaction to see if he looked convinced. When it was done, it looked again at Tom, again with its initial sheepishness and uncertainty, as if to say, "Well?"

Tom was very impressed with the bear at this point, and time had started to go back to normal again. Tom, however, was still incapable of attacking the bear, not because of his initial paralysis, but firstly because he was too in awe of the intense performance he had just witnessed to even remotely consider harming its author, and secondly because he felt that his opportunity had passed and he was no longer in a position to easily kill the bear. But he knew that the bear did not want to harm him, either, so they just stood and stared at each other for a moment, somewhat awkwardly.

It appeared as though the bear was about to meander off down the river when another unexpected thing happened: the bear let out a surprised groan, and looked down at the centre of its chest, through which a metallic screw-like sharp cone was in the process of bloodily drilling. The bear shuddered and spasmed, shook its head around wildly, and then died and fell in a heap on the sand-ledge, revealing behind it a victorious-looking short fellow, just over three feet in height, who wore a tall dirty black top-hat, a dirty brown tailcoat with many odd patches on it opened revealing a brownstained blue-striped button-up shirt, and a pair of very old-looking yellow breeches which looked far too tight to accommodate the requirements of genital comfort. His face was very ugly, protruding where it should flatten and flattening where it should protrude, hideously asymmetrical, and yellow and brown and red and black and blue, irregularly hairy except for a thick moustache which entirely concealed his mouth. His grey-pupilled eyes looked dead, like fisheyes, and they stared straight at Tom with all the grey livid coldness of death. He emanated a strong unpleasant leprous aura, and he exuded a powerful, stale, mildewy odour as though he had just crawled out of a rotten cavern which had been sealed and stagnating for a number of centuries.

Most disturbing to Tom, however, was the feeling, a tingle at the back of his brain, a deep recognition that he had seen this fellow before, that they had some sort of history, the nature of which was muddled and elusive, buried in the foggy backchambers of Tom's mind.

The metallic screw-like object which had impaled the bear was the tip of a long metallic cone about four feet long, ending in a point and widening to a width of about eight inches at the base, with grooves circling around the length of it, which was attached to a small kind of machine from which protruded a wooden handle which the dwarf held very much like a knight would hold his sword after using it long in battle, accomplished and at ease. The short dwarf standing above the huge dead bear with the screw-thing still driven into its back was a memorably bizarre picture: the screw-thing still drilled away in the bear's back, throwing around little bits of bear-gore, and the dwarf's eyelids squinted around their grey vacancies as the dwarf began to speak: he said, from beneath his thick moustache, "I've-been-looking-for-you-sonnyboy-and-I've-been-wanting-to-speak-with-you-aren't-you-glad-I-took-care-of-your-bear-problem-with-my-screwdrill-I-made-it-myself-in-my-basement-where-I-keep-my-tools-and-where-I-keep-my-kittylitterboxes-do-you-like-cats-I've-written-a-poem-this-morning-about-my-favourite-cat-would-you-like-to-hear-it-it's-a-calico-and-it-helps-to-catch-the-mice-would-you-like-to-go-for-a-walk-with-me-I-have-some-important-information-which-it-would-benefit-you-greatly-to-hear-my-lad-don't-worry-it-is-all-for-the-best-bedad-hahahar-let's-go-

I've-got-some-fig-squares-in-my-pocket-in-case-you're-hungry-sure-it-happens-to-the-best-of-us-so-it-does ..." his voice was a rattle, almost incomprehensible, a croak which needed no breath for sustenance but rambled and droned onwards relentlessly and inhumanly like some sort of malevolent noise machine.

The dwarf said many other things also, harmless enough in themselves, but Tom instinctively turned to start running as soon as the dwarf began to speak. However, to his horror he felt at that very moment the ground begin to shake in what was seemingly the beginning of another earthquake, beginning with a slight tremble, which may easily have been a visual trick caused by the vibration of the dwarf's screwdrill, and intensifying throughout the following moments until by the time Tom began to run the earth was shaking violently enough to disrupt his balance and cause him to stagger helplessly as though he had lost control of his legs. Tom managed only to turn his back before the shaking and the weakness proved too much for him and he felt his body begin to sink into the ground, against which motion he fought with every bit of strength he had left in him. The sounds of the earthquake, the rumbling and the explosions, too, began and increased in volume quickly until they became a deafening roar, even worse that it had been in the carriage as it was now coming at him from every direction instead of just one window. The sound hit his head with the heaviness of a cudgel, coming at him from every angle simultaneously creating an unbearable sensation which felt as though he had his head in a vice; his head felt like it was caving in from all directions at once, or like there was an incredible explosive pressure within his skull struggling to get out from everywhere at once. The pressure was greatest in one tiny place, in the lower middle of his forehead, about an inch up from the spot between his eyes, a black dot of enormous agony!

This was not now his main concern, however, much as he disliked it; his only hope was that the dwarf was similarly incapacitated by the earthquake and would not catch up with him. He felt the dwarf's malignant aura behind him, making his skin prickle and his hairs stand up on end and his ears cower. He felt even worse with his back to the dwarf than he had when facing him because he had no idea what the dwarf was doing behind him, and expected the jab of the screwdrill in the small of his back at any moment, but there was nothing to do because he was trapped in mid-air by the shaking and the weakness in his legs, falling slowly, a millimeter per shake, towards the ground. Out of sheer desperation, he tried to call help, but was not sure if he ever made it past the vowel because this too proved impossible, and by then the shaking and the roar were too much for him and his mind finally went blank, dark and blank, and he ceased to feel anything at all.

Part Two

- 6 -
The Return

Tom awoke, like so many other times, yet again on the belly of that fearsome Thing. A cataclysmic crack awakened him; the vice around his skull loosened and let him free again into consciousness. What a dream. What dream? What dream, he asked himself, groaning, lifting his body up with shaking arms, shaking wrists, hands not touching, fingers not feeling anymore. He was awakened by the shaking, which was followed shortly by the rumbling, like explosions in a deep underground cavern, through which he simply could not sleep. How long had he been sleeping, nestled in that warm womb of belly, shaking ravenous belly, quaking monstrous belly? His heart hurt, an achy rawness, and his senses were muddled; his muscles were sore and tired. The Thing had thrown him around and bellowed at him for how long? How much could he endure?

Tom was wet, from sweat probably, no matter whose. And now he knew that the stuff he had thrown into the mouth prior to his nap had been too little indeed. A mere crumb, a mere crumb, no more, for the beast beneath him. A tease, a slight, worse than nothing maybe. The Thing had been calling him, how long? The Thing is angry, hungry. Tom slid down the belly, rolled down the belly, was flung down the belly and landed in a dusty heap on the desert floor.

The noises, too, there all the time. They fall into the background, but not forever, never forever. Notice them, hear them whisper, mumble, speak, hear them coo him, curse him, tell him where to seek.

"Aha!" said Tom to himself, "there it is." The convenient pile of stuff all of which he had not had the energy to throw into the mouth the night before. At least he thought of it as the night before, although he had no sense of day or night in this place. A desert, indeed the landscape did resemble.

Tom crawled towards the pile. Had not there been landscapes in his dream? Rivers, perhaps? The Tigris and the Euphrates he thought fondly to be awaiting him there. Nothing to do but dream in this place, nothing at all.

"Let's make it a good one this time," said Tom, to the Thing. The noises concurred, certainly. He gathered the whole pile of stuff in his arms, and began crawling his way up the side of the Thing, which is no easy task with arms full. Slowly, slowly, a knee at a time, lest he should collapse and drop the stuff and thus negate his efforts.

Noises, of waves, soft lake waters lapping against rock: a storm brewing west of there. Chattering, of birds? A crippled goose lying folded askew at the sandy lakeside croaks. A cat is eying it, a white cat in the bushes: listen, you can hear it lick its lips; its breath disturbs the grass, a rustle, and the goose knows it is there. But the cat doesn't care, for the goose is crippled and its fretting friends have evacuated south. Magnetic severance is a painful thing, but now the goose is alone and helpless. All in good time. At whose door will I leave you tonight? Prrrease accept my gift.

Tom, after making his way slowly and carefully to mid-belly, caught his breath before ascending to the throat. He looked up, saw the wisps, like a congregation of mourning spirits, urging him onwards.

Gunshots rumbled deep in the belly. Artillery barrage: Battle of Waterloo. Napoleon sitting on his horse, Wellington on his. It is too late to win? Curse the mud; curse the water; curse the rain and curse the soul-streaked sky from whence it came. Many more to flit before the day is done. Hear them roar in passing, cursing the bicorned gentlemen; but some, perchance, wish their generals well?

Tom began again, this time towards the throat. There eventually. All in good time. The voices mingling in laughter: have a cigar, you've made it! And then he was there. He dropped the stuff on the throat, picked up a generous handful, and threw it at the mouth.

"Here you go, you soggy shitsmelling mound of filth. I curse the day you were born. I curse your mother, your father, your nasty uncles and your rotten siblings." Tom picked up another handful. "My curse upon you, Thing. I do not feel sorry for you in the slightest. I should cut your throat so you can never bellow at me again; I should leave you here to wither." The voices mingling in cheers and clapping filled the auditorium. There is a storm brewing west of here; I hope it doesn't rain us out. He threw the stuff into the mouth, then bent over and picked up two handfuls. "I hope this satisfies you, my friend. I should locate your genitalia and ruin them."

Soon enough the stuff was gone, the noises quietened, and Tom fell in a heap right where he was, on the throat of that fearsome Thing.

The shaking threw him down the throat to mid-belly, where the comfortable groove was located. The belly's embrace was loving, firm (a little too firm, in fact); and the voices began to sing to him, a pleasant melody in a major key: La-di-dum. La-di-dum. La-di-la-di-dum-dum-dum. Dum-dum-la-di-dum-dum-dum. La-di-dum-dum-dum. And in and out, the wind, the air, the waves, the sea, the notes the whirling melody. Round and round, the sky, the wisps, round and round the melody.

- 7 -
Calpurnia's Tale

Tom was transported immediately back to the riverside, and he was sitting with his back leaned crookedly and uncomfortably up against a tree, facing towards the river. The water reflected the sun blindingly, his head ached and he felt stiff and tired; there was a sharp painful tension in his shoulders and back. He grimaced and tried to lean forward, but then he saw a short shape silhouetted darkly against the river, standing about seven feet before him. Thinking immediately of the dwarf, he fell back involuntarily and hit his head against the tree-trunk, the bark digging sharply into his scalp. Then he felt a pebble hit him in the chest, and heard a voice:

"Hey you!" It was Calpurnia's voice, and her greeting was followed shortly by another pebble, this one hitting him in the stomach.

Tom, achy-headed and confused, leaned forward slowly, and as his eyes adjusted to the light he began to make out Calpurnia's amused face, her yellow shirt and oversized overalls. She was casually throwing a pebble into the air with her right hand and catching it with her left, then reversing the action.

Tom asked anxiously, "The earthquake? The dwarf?"

"The earthquake: it is very unusual for two to happen in one day like that; unheard of, in fact."

Tom rubbed his head, then he asked, "The dwarf?"

"That was a close call, Tom. The dwarf almost got you."

"He didn't get me?" Tom exhaled gratefully, his shoulders slackened, and he fell back onto the tree in relief. After a few moments had passed, during which Calpurnia continued to stare at him amusedly, Tom sat up again and looked at Calpurnia impatiently and said, "All right Calpurnia. How about you tell me what happened? I am having difficulties remembering right now. My head ..." – he brought up his right hand and spread it over his forehead – "is foggy."

"It was quite something to watch. You are very lucky, Tom: you have friends in high places. When I saw the bear I ran away a little bit down the river to let you deal with it. I watched it all at a safe remove from behind a bush downstream." Here she lowered her voice to a whisper and smiled, "Don't worry Tom, your secret's safe with me: Ronny thinks you killed the bear." She then returned to her storytelling tone and continued, "After you killed the bear, the dwarf jumped out of the brambles. It was a terrifying moment: the dwarf came at you, his screwdrill spinning. The earthquake hit right at that moment: you were both paralyzed; the earth shook; trees fell; stones jumped from the riverbank and came hailing down. A pebble hit me on the shoulder!" – she pointed at her right shoulder in disbelief – "The earthquake lasted a few minutes; you both fell. I watched in breathless anxiety to see which of you would get up first. To my horror, the dwarf alone arose. He dusted himself off, picked up his screwdrill, and resumed the approach; you lay unconscious on the ground. Unconscious, is that it?" She paused for a moment and brought her right hand up to her chin and began stroking it thoughtfully, and for a moment resembled Ronny in her pensiveness; after a moment she continued, "You lay on your back, and didn't get up; but your hands groped at the air, and your feet kicked at the ground, like a dog, Tom, just like a dreaming dog. You moron, you didn't get up! You just lay there writhing!" – she brought her fists down on either side of her waist and scowled at Tom indignantly. Then she relaxed her posture and smiled, gaptoothed, and threw her pebble affectionately, hitting Tom in his left shoulder, "And then something amazing happened! You have friends in high places, Tom. As the dwarf approached with murderous intent, a bugle sounded silverly from the trees. Can you believe it, Tom!" She stopped for a moment and looked up at the leaves above Tom's head in wonder, her eyes alight, enchanted by the moment she was recounting; then she continued, more slowly, "A silvery bugle from the trees, and I knew right away it would be all right."

She bent down idly and picked up a pebble, still gazing distractedly at the leaves, and Tom thought he should get up to discourage her from throwing any more pebbles at him. He rose into her gaze and looked at her seriously, "Go on."

She focussed on his face, and continued, somewhat contemptuously, "While you, Tom, were rolling around on the ground like an imbecile, waiting for the dwarf to drill you, the reinforcements arrived. The rescue party: Peter Gardener!"

Tom, his mental faculties slowly returning to him but still achy-headed and muddled, was surprised at this turn in the tale. "Peter Gardener? A rescue party?"

"Yes, Tom, Peter Gardener. Arrows flew out from the trees, landing around the dwarf, discouraging his advance – they didn't hit the dwarf, of course, because he is not to be touched, because of the agreement – the dwarf stopped in midstep and brought his ugly hairy little liverspotted left hand up to his head and clutched it in vexation. Then we saw the glinting of the armour, silvery through the leaves, and we heard the thudding of the boots in the turf, and the dwarf very nearly shat himself –"

"Calpurnia," Tom interrupted, "aren't you a little young to be talking like that?"

Her pebble hit him sharply in his right leg, and she said, "What the hell are you talking about, Tom? Do you want to hear the story or not?"

Tom decided that he deserved this last pebble. "Sorry, Calpurnia, I'm still a little achy."

"And stupid, right; what should I expect? Would you like some water?" she gestured at the river. "There is no shortage at the moment."

Tom thought this was probably a good idea. He staggered unsteadily towards the water, but he encountered a problem when he arrived at the edge of the riverbank and realized that because of the steepness of the slope, dropping four feet down to the water, he could not lean over to drink. He stood puzzled for a moment, stroking his chin, and then to his great surprise he felt Calpurnia's little hands pushing him hard in his lower back; as he fell into the river, he heard her say, "Get in there, you big stupid moron!"

He flopped into the water, his arms and legs waving about helplessly. Luckily the river was shallow by the bank. He picked himself up, overwhelmed by the sudden chill of the water, and looked up at her angrily; he was about to berate her but when he saw her face rippling in laughter, a face mischievous but guileless, he was drained of his ire.

"Wake up, mister!"

Tom laughed and bent down to pick up some water with the cup of his two hands. He felt much more awake now, the shock of the cold water and the adrenaline release caused by the fall having forced the necessary sharpening of his senses.

Calpurnia went on with her story. "As the archers charged out from the trees, three longboats came around the bend, bugles blaring silverly, full of bearded men-at-arms ready to do battle. They sang their warsong, a deep intimidating Dorian murmur, and the dwarf turned aghast at the sound of them. He dropped his screwdrill, it turned off with a sputter, and he brought his right hand up to his head, grabbed his top-hat, and threw it onto the rocks. 'Run away, pukesack! Go back to your basement, wormcrotch!' shouted the formidable warriors."

As Calpurnia told the story and Tom drank the riverwater with closed eyes, something very interesting began to happen: he began to see with a sparkling vividness the events described; he could see the bearded, broached warriors in their longboats, staring contemptuously through the slits of their eyes from under their Norse helmets, their upper lips curled defiantly as they cursed the illshaped dwarf; he saw their polished chainmail glinting, their longswords waving threateningly in the air. He could feel the wind, the excitement; he could hear the sounds of their jeers, their song, the dip of the oars in the water, the grunts of the oarsmen, and the pound and rustle of the archers' boots in the woods. He began to experience the events unfolding as Calpurnia told them simultaneously as though her narration was accompanying his vision and not vice-versa.

"But that was not all. From both directions came the horsemen along the riverbank, completing the trap; the dwarf had nowhere to run. They were so beautiful: gleaming chainmail, polished helmets, shining horses, grimly handsome knights come to the rescue, hoofbeats like thunder," Tom saw and heard it all, suspended above the scene like a hawk. "The dwarf froze, and began gnawing on his fingernails. He pissed himself, causing the warriors to jeer all the more. In a moment, the men-at-arms in the longboats disembarked and swarmed onto the riverbank, the archers formed a line at the edge of the forest, and the knights circled the dwarf, the dead bear, and your helpless self. Peter Gardener himself was there, unarmed on his horse, Petunia, and he approached the dwarf, who dropped to his knees and threw his arms up in surrender. Then Peter turned and addressed the warriors,

"'Comrades, I have composed a song for this occasion:

'The dawn is bright;
Odin-hawk in flight
is watching.

The foe is weak,
and poor, and small
in stature; we should be back
in time for brunch.'

"Then, turning again to the dwarf, he said, 'What do you think you're doing, Donald? You know you're supposed to leave Tom alone. You should stay in your corner of the world, Donald; don't go interfering.'

"The dwarf began rambling incomprehensibly and shaking his head about like it was on fire, his breeches wet from piss and tears of fear streaming down his face."

"Yes," said Tom quietly, "I see."

"'Get up, Donald,' said Peter Gardener, and the dwarf rose. 'Pick up your hat.' The dwarf picked up his top-hat. 'Pick up your screwdrill.' The dwarf picked up his screwdrill. 'Now begone! Back to your little corner, Donald; back to your basement.'

"The warriors laughed deeply amongst themselves, and opened a lane for the dwarf to pass; some of them kicked him in his ass or spat on him or cursed and insulted him. The dwarf scampered away into the trees, his head bowed pathetically. The men-at-arms began to get back into their longboats; the archers disappeared into the woods; only the knights remained in a circle around you and the dead bear. I stood up and came out from the bushes, and Peter Gardener told me, 'Hello, my dear Calpurnia. This was a close call. Make sure our Tom here gets some bear into him quickly, and let him know what a close call this was, and how lucky he is.' Then he gave me some chocolate and told me to keep it all for myself, and they left! So there it is, Tom, the story of your misadventure."

"I see," said Tom. The water of the river tasted good: the liquid seemed to spread through his whole body to every extremity instantaneously as he swallowed it, refreshing his core, revitalizing his limbs, turning his flesh into a coating of humming aquatic coolness, and jolting his insides with a sharp shiver of electricity. His eyes still closed, he drank until his mouth froze and his teeth hurt and he could stomach no more, watching from up high the rescue party disperse and the dwarf slink away through the trees; then he opened his eyes to a world infinitely richer in colour and sharper in detail than that which he had left prior to falling into the river. He looked up at Calpurnia, who looked strangely cool, confident and collected on the riverbank, and said, "Thank you for that, Calpurnia; you are a true friend." He stretched long and youngly, then said, "I don't know about you, Calpurnia, but I am damn hungry. Where's Ronny?"

- 8 -
The Sparrow's Poem

Tom crawled up the slope of the riverbank, and when he made it to the top he saw Ronny leaning over the dead bear with his customary air of assured self-importance, flanked on either side by George and another young man who was similarly attired and physically similar except that he had longish brown hair instead of George's short blonde hair. Tom was glad Ronny thought that he had killed the bear, and he made an effort to look level-headed, composed and successful.

As he approached the three Ronny turned to him and said, "You really know how to take care of a bear. Very efficient indeed. This fellow never had a chance!" Ronny laughed loudly and clapped Tom on the shoulder. "Good job, Tom; Mother will be very pleased." This thought pleased Tom; things had turned out very well indeed. He smiled and nodded; then Ronny gestured at the bear's body and said, "I see you know about $T4$."

This surprised Tom, as he had absolutely no idea what $T4$ was, and it reminded him of HP, another thing of which he had no understanding; but, again not wanting to reveal his lack of hunting experience, he continued to nod and smile, adding after a moment, "But of course."

"It is hard to get the $T4$, because you must sneak up from behind and not make a sound, not to mention the superhuman strength required." He looked Tom up and down in amazement, "I didn't know you had it in you! I've never seen anybody make use of the $T4$ technique until today. It is a very thorough way to kill: not only do you kill the animal, but you also kill all of its offspring simultaneously; you undo its entire existence in one stroke, and ensure that its children will not come after you at a later date. Not only that: it also undoes everything the animal has ever done, every action no matter how small, as well as every action of the animal's offspring, as if the animal never existed at all, leaving only the organic matter in its current state. A bit excessive in this case, I think," – he looked at Tom somewhat reproachfully – "but very impressive nonetheless."

Tom at this moment was overcome by yet another wave of disbelief and incomprehension, all the more dizzying for its temporal proximity to his moment of triumph. What on earth was Ronny talking about? Were he not so lightheaded from incomprehension, Tom would have felt even sorrier for the bear for the simultaneous death of all its offspring, but he had not at that moment yet registered this warped information enough to begin thinking about it rationally.

After a long moment, Tom said, "Well, you know, one likes to be thorough," and the three boys laughed. George and the other young man looked at Tom with admiration and respect, and friendly curiosity, and Tom felt that this couldn't be a bad thing and was encouraged to continue in his bluff: "I just threw a pebble over its shoulder when it was looking down; it looked up in the direction of the noise, and I struck. It was all over in a second: the bear felt no pain." Tom crouched and laid his hand on the bear's fur. It was warm from the sun, and seemed rather too clean and soft for a wild animal. "It was a mighty bear, a rare bear. But now it is dead and we shall eat it for lunch," Tom said quietly, although he did not have any particular reason for admiring the bear so much, because he could not remember the events surrounding his meeting the bear but was only familiar with it as it was in its current, dead, state. But nonetheless he felt very sorry for the bear, and did not at all want to eat it, but his comrades mistook his sorrow for heroic solemnity and said nothing.

After a few moments, George took some rope out of the duffel bag and gave the other young man a hatchet which the other took and walked over to a thick sapling at the edge of the woods and began chopping it down. Tom considered that this recent success with the bear had landed him in a rather superior position in the esteem of these young people, which struck him as advantageous. He looked over at Calpurnia, feeling thankful for her friendship, but she was throwing pebbles into the river and singing to herself. Ronny was still studying the bear in fascination, muttering at intervals, "A most remarkable thing ... a perfect textbook $T4$ execution ... He didn't even damage any meat." Suddenly he clapped his hands together and said, happily, "It is decided. You can stay, Tom. You are one of us now."

Tom patted the bear softly and stood, "Thank you, Ronny. I promise you will not regret your decision. As you know, I forage, fish, hunt, build and explore superbly. Your people will be enriched to no end." Tom strolled away upriver as he said this, leaving the young men to their work and Calpurnia with her pebbles.

Tom looked around. Every incident which had occurred since his first seeing the bear – the dwarf, the earthquake – had been unexpected, stressful, and therefore also rather physically arduous. Tom could not pinpoint precisely the effects of these incidents on his mind or body, but he felt a general kind of shock. The water he had drunk from the river had refreshed and stimulated him, sharpened his sensations and allowed him to think clearly and respond adequately, but it had also caused him to feel more acutely the shock caused by these recent incidents. This shock left him feeling only half-present.

However, no sooner had he realized the extent of this shock than he realized that this was not the most prominent sensation he was feeling at this moment. As he looked around, he saw the beauty of the trees and the magic of the water and how the rays of the sun complemented it all, just as he had when he had been walking along the path with Calpurnia earlier and they had stopped to enjoy the view from the cliff, but there was something else now.

Tom considered more closely his present sensations. Earlier he had felt connected to and firmly settled in the world which surrounded him. He had felt essentially whole and undivided. The rich shimmering beauty of the world had mirrored and nourished a richness and wholeness of being within his own breast, in a kind of satisfying exchange. Now, however, he was keenly aware of cataclysmic juxtapositions, irreconcilable forces, within his own self, mirroring similar cleavages in the outer world which had earlier seemed so sound and complete. Furthermore, he felt that while earlier he was being pulled along a trajectory already mapped out for him, now he felt like this pull had been somehow interiorized and transformed into powerful physiological imperatives, pushing him with their own force.

He was hungry, among other things, but his hunger did not feel like he had earlier expected it to feel. Indeed, he was quite certain that it was entirely unlike any hunger he had ever before experienced; he only labeled it "hunger" for want of a better noun. He felt like there was a ball of intense energy seated deep in his gut. It was not any kind of nausea, and did not feel bad; rather it was a kind of vibrating presence which could not be ignored; it was like a humming ball of infinite tension. It was concentrated in his gut, but it sent powerful shockwaves pulsating throughout his limbs at irregular but frequent intervals, making him twitch and fidget and kick at the pebbles as he thought. It extended its vibrations into his chest, making it contract, and it spread into the muscles of his back, legs and arms, making them flex and tighten. His jaws were clenched like a vice; his masseters were like tautened bundles of wires stretched near breaking point; his whole body trembled like a rod possessed by a terrific electricity. He felt like this force would send him writhing in spasms on the ground if he did not find a way to either calm or unleash it. The hum in his gut was the realest thing to him at this moment: it was far realer than the papery trees or the dull weight of his flesh and bones.

As for the outer world, the riverbank, the trees, the leaves, the clouds, and the birds all shared a common aura of unreality: they looked like they had been cut out of paper and painted with impressively consistent uniformity of style, as though the artist was either impervious to exhaustion or had an infinite amount of time in which to pay attention to detail, but this very uniformity of style reinforced the blatant aura of unreality. It seemed even as if the objects didn't bother being there at all when he wasn't looking at them and threw themselves up at the last moment before he turned his head to fix them with his focus. Tom tried to ignore this aura of unreality, but it nagged at him with a kind of unsettling intentionality all of its own. His thought had a crystalline clarity to it, but it seemed to reject every object it came across as superfluous and unimportant, making in turn itself, consciousness itself, seem objectless and superfluous. And his thought seemed to partake of the hum in his belly its own ample share.

In opposition to the papery unreality of solid objects, the water possessed a quality of heaviness which seemed almost to create its own gravitational pull. Recognizing this, Tom realized with a sudden flash of understanding the cause of his sensations: it was the water! The water passed downwards through his system, collected in his belly, spread outwards, transforming, vibrating, sending bolts through his spine like an electric storm. It tightened his muscles, straightened his back, sent him into shivers. It was pulling him downwards, towards the ground, towards the river; he felt like he would end up curled up in a little ball in the riverbed, one with the water, if he would only let the water pull him there.

Perhaps the most striking thing about these intense sensations was that he couldn't decide which was more alien to him: his body or the force it confined. On the one hand, he felt markedly disconnected from the matter which seemed so unreal; his own body felt like a kind of heavy anchor and, in a way, he felt like he had more in common with the unfathomable void of sky than with this burdensome shell. But on the other hand he felt attached inseparably to the heaviness of matter, of his body; he felt that this was all there was, in a sense, aside from the cool electricity of the water and, even more, the emptiness of sky, and he feared the thought of losing it and being cast out into liquid or ethereal freedom. For he was at once both and neither.

Tom interpreted all this as hunger because he felt intuitively that to eat something would calm, if only temporarily, this overwhelming humming tension caused by the water. He knew that he would have to deal with it again eventually, writhe again under its influence, but he knew also that a sufficient amount of bear meat would mask it once more as the calm, even energy that concentrated in his breast rather than in his gut, and which harmoniously coexisted with and basked amid, rather than rebelled against, the solid world of matter. He then thought of Mother, her light brown hair, her full breasts and wide hips, her fair skin in the dark room, and her gleaming eyes; the thought of her, following his thought of food as a predictable connection, flashed across his consciousness with a jolt, and he kicked at the pebbles at his feet compulsively and clenched his jaws the tighter.

Suddenly, a swallow darted down diagonally from the trees and landed a few paces before him and began strutting back and forth and jerking its head to and fro in usual birdy fashion. It strutted around, making circles, squares, triangles, pentagons, hexagons, and many more complex geometrical shapes which have no names, on the rocky riverbank before Tom with bewildering speed, until the frenetic rhythms of the humming electricity in Tom's body began mirroring its dance, at first in clumsy imitation, and then in perfect mimicry as though they were fused together. Once the fusion had been firmly established, the bird stopped and looked up at Tom. The bird's eyes were tiny little black beads, but Tom perceived a clear and unmistakeable expression in them, which he could only recognize as a kind of stunned, disbelieving bafflement. Then the bird surprised Tom by speaking; the voice was that of a young man, not too deep, a confident, youthful tenor. The swallow said,

"Before My Eyes, or A Familiar Kind of Morning

"Talon-branches grasp whiteflecked sky
like a gardener's warm, worn paper hands.
Serene and bold, a lone bird flies,
though in the wrong direction.

"In eastern ether, a sharp pink gash:
slightest slit of warmest sunflash.
A promise too ardent to be spoken aloud
yet is vanishing anyhow.

"A silence settled beneath the clouds
Upon a much-warmed Maytime morn.

Stirred, a heart throbs fast and loud
for the silence is so cold.

"Before my eyes? Whose eyes if not mine?
What chains me to this, the same old ground?
Chained too to wings Mad Destiny lends;
    and I left to wonder to what odd ends
    this familiar trajectory tends."

The swallow seemed to wink at Tom, and then he took off in the opposite direction from whence he had come, over the river towards the other, east side.

- 9 -
Ronny's Speculations

Tom turned back to the group and saw that the sapling had been felled, its branches pulled off, and brought over to the bear's body where George and Ronny were tying the bear's forelegs and hindlegs together respectively. When they were done, the other young man, whom Tom heard George call by the name of Jack, then proceeded to take the sapling and insert its thinner end between the bear's forelegs and then through his hindlegs, this being the chosen method of transportation. After the sapling had been thus placed, all three boys looked up at Tom as he approached.

Tom said, "Well, fellas, I am getting awfully hungry."

They nodded in agreement, saying they were hungry also. Ronny called Calpurnia away from her pebble-throwing, and George and Jack each picked up an end of the sapling, suspending the bear's weight between them in the familiar fashion. Though they were both well-built, they struggled under the weight of the bear. Tom did not feel inclined to help, and watched them as they encountered difficulties in traversing the little hill on the other side of which lay the path, as it was fairly steep and covered in trees and bushes. It took them a while, as they often tripped and slid backwards down the slope under the awkward weight of the bear, but they were adamant and made it far quicker than Tom had expected they would, due to their youthful athletic determination. They did not reproach Tom for not helping them, for he had done enough already, and they were only too happy to show off their abundant zeal; and Tom was probably not even capable of being particularly helpful because of the hum in his stomach. They had difficulty again going down the other side, but they had gravity on their side this time, and eventually they slid down in a pile into the little ditch, picked themselves up, and made it to the path, where they stopped, flushed and laughing, to catch their breath, Tom, Ronny and Calpurnia sliding down after them.

After a moment, the five of them began walking up along the small path back towards the carriage. Ronny fell into step with Tom and said, "So I heard you had a run-in with Donald?"

"Donald?" Tom said, wondering as to the details of the version of the story Ronny had. "Yes, he caught me by surprise. Do you know him?"

"Everyone in this area knows about Donald Murchader," said Ronny.

"Oh," said Tom. "What does he want with me?"

Ronny squinted in consideration of this question; after a moment, he said, "I don't know, Tom; I have no idea. Maybe Father would know; maybe that's what that was all about." He shrugged, "I'll try to ask him later if he knows anything about it."

They walked on a bit more in silence, Tom feeling the tension in his belly increase incrementally at every step, and then Ronny said, "I've never met the dwarf. He usually stays in his corner, down by the bay."

Tom, despite the distraction in his belly, wanted to learn more about Donald Murchader, now that the subject had been introduced. He said, "What's his story?"

Ronny smirked a little, "His biography?"

"Yes," said Tom, "his biography, if you are in a position to help me in this regard."

Ronny nodded. "I am familiar with Donald's biography. It is not particularly complicated. He lives by the bay, located northwest of here, where we found you this morning. The reason that his biography is so uncomplicated is that he has been there for as long as anybody can remember ... He's been here even longer than Peter Gardener! Or whoever Peter Gardener works for." He stroked his chin in the customary fashion.

Tom was not satisfied with this explanation; he had wanted to hear something which would help explain the dwarf's malignant repulsiveness. This description of the dwarf as having always been here only increased this disturbing sense of malignancy. "So that's all there is to it, then?" asked Tom, somewhat uneasily.

"What more could you want?" asked Ronny. But Tom knew from his voice that he was being clever again, and was holding back. Thus Tom didn't reply, trying to make it clear with his silence that he wanted Ronny to speak plainly. Finally, Ronny complied, "Well, Tom. It is an interesting and difficult question you ask. Why is he so hideous, and evil? Why is he such a grotesque little character? Why do we despise him on first sight and not expend the slightest bit of sympathy on him? These are profound questions. A stray dog – and we have many stray dogs in these parts – may be wretched, emaciated, mangy. But beneath its disease-ridden exterior we see the poor, deprived soul peeking out at us, and we separate, in our minds, its repulsive, stinky sores from its innocent soul, and we are no longer so entirely put off by its mangy hide. We feel sorry for it, and empathize with it, understanding that anybody could end up in a similar state in similar circumstances. While not everyone is able to completely overcome this repulsion, we all have the capability in varying degrees. We can separate the animal's inherent healthiness and innocence of spirit from the circumstances of its wretchedness, and see beyond this wretchedness. But not so with Donald Murchader."

Tom felt that Ronny was driving right to the core of the matter. He nodded in agreement and said, "Quite right: no so with the dwarf."

"Well, Tom. That is as far as I wish to pursue the matter. I have never met Mr Murchader, as you are already aware, nor am I interested in ever meeting him. But from what I have heard from others who have seen him, he is a very repulsive little fellow and he is not at all to be trusted, or helped, or sympathized with. I can only guess that he is somehow inherently pestilential, awry, misbegotten. He must be afflicted with a very sickness of soul, or of genes, so innate that it occupied a moment of ultimate precedence in the assemblage of his being. He is a kind of walking curse, not to mention his notorious addiction to killing. In other words, Tom, at no time in Mr Murchader's existence was he in possession of the same innocence of soul and body of which we are all in possession upon first entering the world, and which we lose at various rates and for various reasons due to our choices and circumstances. He never had it to begin with: he was born a wretch and he will die a wretch. An anhedonic monstrosity to be avoided at all costs. He is a very manifestation of negativity, having nothing to share with the world but this negativity –" Ronny seemed to be getting excited, and he suddenly stopped himself and looked at Tom apologetically, "But I've gone too far in my speculations: I've never even met the man. For all I know, he is a very nice chap and everyone has been misunderstanding the poor fellow entirely."

Tom did not think this was the case. "And what about this agreement, that he is not to be touched, that Calpurnia was talking about?"

"Oh, Tom, I don't know. Such things go back well before my time. There must be some good reason. I suppose I could ask Father if you want."

They walked on a bit more in silence. Tom knew that they were approaching the carriage, recognizing the path from earlier. The day was getting warmer, and Tom judged from the position of the sun that it must be getting close to noon. The water was still doing its strange things in his stomach, not calming down at all, and throughout Ronny's speech he felt the tension sitting in there, responding in its own way to Ronny's words, reflecting his reactions with its own system of aquatic semiotics. He was becoming somewhat accustomed to the idea of carrying around this tension in his belly, but the shivering and gyrating which it sent throughout his body was by its very nature not something to which one could become accustomed. He decided to ask about lunch. "How long before we can get eating, Ronny? I am getting rather hungry."

"In under an hour. We just need to get back to the house and cook it. We are all hungry. It is lucky that you got us the bear, Tom, as today is the Summer Solstice, and we are going to have a party."

Tom was not interested in this last piece of news, as it had nothing to do with eating. He did not even stop to consider that the sparrow had either gotten his date wrong, or was reciting a poem he had written several weeks earlier. Had he stopped to consider this, he may have ended up noticing that when he had first stepped foot from the castle earlier to speak with Peter Gardener it had felt like spring and throughout the morning the season had nearly imperceptibly progressed, along with the hour, until by now, approaching noon, it felt very much like midsummer. But Tom did not notice this at all; he noticed only that the temperature was rising steadily, but there was a watery hum in his gut which was keeping him cool. After a time, he said, "Summer Solstice, eh? I am feeling very horny – I mean hungry," and in fact he was both.

They finally arrived at the carriage, and George and Jack somehow (Tom had stopped looking at them) managed to get the bear on top of the carriage, its forelegs and hindlegs still tied around the sapling. After storing away the weapons, George and Jack went into the booth with the duffel bag and shut the door, and Ronny, Calpurnia and Tom returned to their places in the driver's seat. They then began clopping back the way they had come.

The ride back to the the house was a flash, as Tom was no longer in the same voyeuristic mood in which he had been earlier on the ride to the river, but was rather possessed wholly by the bodily tumult caused by the hum in his stomach, which did not fade, but rather increased in intensity. He was beginning to sweat from the heat. His facial expressions, as they were regarded by some onlookers of the animal and bird kingdoms who happened to look up as the carriage was passing, were intense and gargoyle-like, indicative of extreme tension. His lower jaw moved round and round in a hypnotic rhythm which haunted many onlookers for days afterwards in their dreams and subconscious waking thoughts; his eyeballs bulged out from their sockets as though they were being pushed out by some incredible pressure, which indeed they were; his nostrils flared; his eyelids were peeled wide open, and his brow was pulled up in a fixed configuration expressive of astonished overstimulation; his hands were clenched whiteknuckled around the railing in front of the seat. All exterior objects, abandoned for their unreality by his perception, had become alike blurry. Every muscle, tightened, was hard as steel, and he shook the carriage with a vibration which only just went unnoticed by his comrades. They sped through the town and into the driveway of the house in what felt to Tom like a matter of seconds.

- 10 -
The Solstice Party

As the carriage went down the road towards the house, about twenty people in the front yard, many of the same that had been there earlier and similarly engaged, leapt up and down in welcoming glee. "Good job, Tom! What a hero! He's the Solstice Hero!"

Tom was happy to hear them say these things, but he did not smile, unable to share in their lightness of spirit because of the hefty hum in his belly and the tension it spread through every muscle, and he said, through clenched teeth, "It was no problem, really, nothing to fuss about."

After they had disembarked, Tom found himself at the centre of a group of admiring young people, all of whom seemed to be between the ages of four and twenty-four, dressed irregularly but all somehow similarly unremarkable. None were unattractive, and all were healthy-looking, but that their appearance was so uniformly fresh turned this freshness into a bland mediocrity, also largely due to the current unreality of solid things. They all said things to him, and Tom answered some of them, but he was not aware of what either he or they were saying. There were hands on him, some of them stroking and groping him sensually, but he was only aware of the bear being lugged off the roof of the carriage by George, Jack and few other young fellows and carried out of sight into the back yard. He followed the bear, pushing through the people, pleading with them, agreeing with them, thanking them, even apologizing, and the mass of bodies grudgingly budged slowly towards the back yard. Then he was aware of a voice, louder than the others, in his right ear, the voice of a young man, deep and demanding,

"Mr Tom, I have a few questions about the T4 technique. No-one around here has ever used it before, and I thought that since you are something of an expert on the matter you could shed some light on a few things for me. For instance, it is said that the T4 technique undoes every action that the animal has ever done, as well as every action all of its offspring have ever done, et cetera, ad infinitum, but what does that mean for every meal? I mean, say you jabbed the T4 on a brontosaurus, and this brontosaurus had eaten a tree, would the tree go back to the way that it was before the brontosaurus had eaten it? But how would that work? If a person were to take a nap where a brontosaurus had eaten a tree fifty years earlier, and you did the T4 on this brontosaurus right at that moment, would the tree return to that place, possibly injuring the person who is sleeping there? In other words, does the being which is created in the vacuum left by the animal's meal suffer destruction by the undoing of the meal, or is it safely displaced? Presumably not, because logically the undoing of the brontosaurus' meal would also undo the person's having been able to sleep there in the first place, causing the person to take a nap elsewhere, presenting the hypothetical scenario wherein one might go to a field and take a nap somewhere and wake up five minutes later three feet to the left of a large tree occupying the spot where one had fallen asleep five minutes earlier. The destructive act of a T4 execution is, therefore, also necessarily a creative, as well as a restorative, act. But there is another question which intrigues me far more: say the animal says something to someone, and influences this person to make certain decisions in his or her life, are these words undone by the T4 execution? What is the situation with metaphysical actions? Do you see the implications? What happens to that person when the words which influenced him or her so many years since are undone? If someone had found Lord Henry Wotton ten years after the death of Dorian Gray, and done the T4 on him, would Dorian have become, not as he was before he spoke to Lord Henry, but a completely different person, the result of the lack of Lord Henry's influence? It is hard to imagine, a heck of a conundrum, and it leads one to wonder what this means about metaphysical action, and also causes one to realize that the line we draw between physical and metaphysical action becomes blurred in situations like this. In certain situations, would not the whole world suddenly change in an instant? How could it not? And would we be aware of this change? I think not –"

"Well, my friend, it sounds to me like you just answered your own questions," said Tom. "And, what is more, you think like a twit; I have encountered finer thought in sparrows," he added, not at all aware of the words he was speaking, pushing his way through the crowd.

"But there is something that doesn't make sense. Wouldn't that undo the very doing of the T4 in the first place, somehow, owing to the interconnectedness of all things?" Tom pushed past the voice, and heard it call after him, "Oh, by the way, sir, did you ever consider that you may be the Anti-Christ?"

"No! I most certainly did not! Quite the contrary, in fact, for I am the Solstice Hero!"

Tom was then aware of another voice, that of a young woman, "Mr Tom, you are very tense. I could help you with that. Why don't you let the boys cook up a meal and we can go for a walk?" Tom looked at the young woman: she had black hair, was attractive in a well-fed way, and she smiled seductively at him, taking hold of his sweaty hand. She said, "You are, after all, the Solstice Hero."

Tom growled, "Thank you, madam, but it is absolutely imperative that I eat something first," and he shed her hand and pushed his way through the crowd.

Tom heard more voices, all directed at him, all friendly in intent but oppressive in result. He felt the bodies close in on him and several hands fall upon him, and then he felt himself being lifted off the ground by the hands and into the air until he was facing the sky. He heard them chanting below him, "Tom the Solstice Hero! Tom the Solstice Hero!"

At this moment the hum became too much for him and he lost control over his muscles. He felt the watery hum overpower his body entirely, turning it into a buzzing aqueous jelly that shook and vibrated in the hands of the people below. The clouds whizzed by with remarkable speed, white puffs soaring across the unfathomable blue, and Tom was blissfully disembodied. He had stopped fighting the hum, had merged with the hum, had become the hum; the vibrations regularized until he felt at one with the clouds above, like they were all tuned to the same great aquatic pulse, a euphoric wave.

Tom was not aware of what happened over the next short while. The great pulse cast its spell, and Tom and the clouds reveled in their common wateriness for some considerable time. He was carried around by the chanting crowd for nearly half an hour, and finally his body was laid at the foot of a tree. Then George smilingly brought over a plate of bear meat from where it had been cooking on a bonfire in the middle of the yard, and he cut off a piece and considered how best to get the incapacitated Tom to open his mouth. He decided to poke Tom in the belly, this part of him seeming to be the tensest. He poked Tom in the belly with his right forefinger, and Tom emitted a grunt and his left leg spasmed wildly. George poked Tom again, and Tom opened his mouth to tell him to go to hell and he deftly inserted the piece of meat between Tom's teeth.

As the meat entered Tom's mouth, he was overwhelmed by a new set of sensations. His jaws closed mechanically on the meat, his anticipating saliva leapt on it predatorily, and he felt the juices of the meat spread through his mouth like fire. His eyes shot open, and he grabbed the meat with both hands and proceeded to devour it fiercely. His body awoke zestfully from its watery stupor, and his insides churned into digestive action all at once. The meat made much of itself: it had a very strong woody flavour, and the spicy juices sparked his digestive channels into new life with shocks and prickles. The meat was very tough, and the digestion thereof sucked all of Tom's electric watery energy and transformed it directly into a heavy, satisfied fullness.

He finished the meat, and before he could even look up to locate the bonfire George heaped another large piece of bear meat onto his plate, as well as some lettuce and a cucumber. Tom devoured it all just as quickly, and found a bowl filled with water at his right side, which he picked up and gulped down in a few short seconds. The water had a completely different effect on him now that it was complemented by the meat: the two worked together, sending waves of thick pleasure throughout Tom's nerves, making him feel like a great joy-producing machine. His vision was a blur, and he was not at all shy about being so gluttonous in front of so many people, because to him they were not there.

After he could eat no more, Tom folded his hands behind his head, lay back on the foot of the tree, and stared up at the long crooked leafy branches of the tree and the sky beyond. The sky was changing: grey clouds were pushing in from the west, covering the sun with dark grasping paws, and it looked like it would soon rain. Tom noticed that the air was humid and heavy, increasing his sluggishness. Tom closed his eyes, and something interesting began to happen. Images, which had faded into the backdrop of his mind since Calpurnia's tale, cast aside by his consciousness as irrelevant and unhelpful, but which had nonetheless lingered like the ticking of a clock, unnoticed yet ever-present, became sharper and more prominent, until they occupied the centre-stage of his imagination, shifting and swirling with their own independent volition. He saw the face of the bear, its dead eyes staring vacantly, a ghastly furry non-entity. Tom recognized the bear as the same that George and Jack had carried onto the carriage, brought back to the house, had cooked and fed to him, but he felt that there was an incompleteness to his memory. It was like a wall of blankness, standing abruptly in his mind and blocking him from accessing certain memories contained therein. He knew something was missing, that something was behind that wall, but every time he tried thinking back to the events surrounding his first meeting the bear there was this wall of blankness stopping him in his tracks. The bear's head lay dead on the ground, framed by the pebbles of the sand ledge, unknown, unknowable. Tom was too comfortably filled with bear meat, however, to worry about blank spots in his memory, and anyway, his daydream had its own inexorable plot, for the pebble-framed bear's head gradually turned into Father's head floating in the green bubbly fluid, his eyeballs fluttering. What is he dreaming? What will he think when he wakes? A nasty thing, surely, to wake bodiless, floating in a green fluid. But presumably he could be euthanized if he wanted – surely his family would be merciful if he asked them – and therefore he must enjoy being a bodiless head in a bottle of green fluid. Maybe he feels good. The head floated, the eyeballs fluttered, amid slowly spinning panoramas of beautiful valleys, wide lakes, empty deserts, luscious forests, tall palaces with hanging gardens, towers on mountaintops, tropical islands on warm bluegreen seas, and then they returned again to the bland white closet and, much to Tom's surprise, Father's eyes suddenly opened and immediately fixed their gaze on Tom: Father's eyes were angry, vengeful, possessed by wild fury. His mouth opened and he started shouting at Tom accusingly, but Tom could not hear what he said or read his lips; he knew only that

Father was angry with him and wished him no good. Tom felt like Father thought he had done something terrible, something forbidden by the forefathers, and he knew that he must suffer for it for there was no forgiveness in Father's eyes. Father's mouth started moving quicker and quicker, heaping accusations on Tom with exponentially increasing speed, each one graver than the last, until Tom felt the weight of the accusations like an anvil on his chest. "I'm sorry! Just let me go and I will never think of this place again!" But then Father smiled, and his green wrinkled lips became Mother's full young lips, entreating him with offerings of tours of the house and bear meat and more, smilingly paying him compliments and promises. Tom was overcome by thankfulness, and nodded and smiled appreciatively, basking in the radiance of her soft fair skin, her smooth brown hair, warmed by the tantalizing prospect of her full breasts and wide hips; the flowers on her dress bobbed and danced bluely, spreading and stretching themselves revealingly over the curves of her body, inviting irresistibly. He could not hear her words, but he knew that she was saying things he would be happy to hear. He smiled and nodded, nodded and smiled, until his whole body was shaking up and down in grateful affirmation. Someone was shaking him.

"Wake up, Tom! Something terrible has happened in the house!"

Tom, now long recovered from the paralysis caused by the watery hum, physically harmonious and complete from the consumption of the bear meat and mentally recharged by the daydream he had had during digestion, opened his eyes and saw that he was surrounded by the same crowd which had stifled and carried him around earlier, only now they looked at him quietly and expectantly, as though they needed him. Ronny was kneeling at his right, and was shaking him with his hands on his two shoulders. "Really? I thought people weren't allowed inside, except in rare circumstances," exclaimed Tom in surprise.

"They're not!" said Ronny with a broken voice.

Once Tom's eyes had fully awakened, they focussed on Ronny's face, Tom having detected a hitherto unfamiliar tone of fear, even horror, which surprised him. Ronny was trembling; tears streamed down his face, and although he was not crying at that moment Tom could tell that he had just been sobbing uncontrollably. His eyes were filled with that high horror which only a child can feel (one who can imagine anything but never expects it to actually happen, as opposed to the adult who always unimaginatively expects the worst) and the myriad possibilities suggested by his horrified eyes flooded Tom's consciousness with a dark fantastic wave. But Ronny said nothing, too stunned by his horror to speak about it; so finally Tom said, "What is it, Ronny? Have courage!"

"Mother ..." his lips trembled, and his breath hissed through his mucous-covered teeth, "Mother ... is decapitated!"

Tom sat up with a start to better ingest this momentous and unexpected piece of information. "Ronny, surely you don't mean to tell me that Mother has been decapitated? How can this be?" Ronny nodded tragically and covered his mouth with both hands and sobbed explosively into them. Tom did not fully believe that Mother had been decapitated – rather, he did not want to believe it. The news did not horrify Tom as it did Ronny, but he was quite disappointed in a somewhat childish way, as one who is winning a game is disappointed when one is no longer winning, and this in turn caused him not to believe the news with a kind of stubborn denial. He wanted to go back to his daydream and wake up another way, to a different, happier piece of information – Mother was ready to show him around the house, for instance. "Well, that's a pity," said Tom.

Ronny said, "It was the girl! We need to find her! Everybody, grab a weapon and spread out!" He leapt up, suddenly in a blind hyperactive rage, and began shouting instructions, "George and Jack, take the carriage and make a perimeter around Meade, down Academy, up Queen, up Wilson and back to Meade, then open outwards; Gordon, Stacey, Susie, Margaret, Greg, Dave, John, Tim, Sam, Jim, Patricia, Alex, Isabelle, and Erin search the houses on the block, quickly!; Don, Cassandra, Natalie, Simone, Anne, Walter, Ophelia, Louis, Julia, Kathleen, Bob, everybody else! On foot, spread out, take a weapon, and bring her back alive! If you're under sixteen, take an older partner! Ditto if you're a girl under eighteen. If you're under thirteen, stay in the yard until we come back." The whole crowd dispersed in an instant, everyone apparently sharing Ronny's eagerness to find the girl, except the younger ones who huddled in a few talkative circles. Then Ronny turned to Tom and said, "You come with me! We're going to search the house."

Tom rose and followed the excited boy. As they left the shelter of the tree, Tom felt a raindrop hit him on his right arm and he realized that a much-needed rain had begun to fall, for it was extremely humid. The rain intensified quickly as they went to the carriage, the rear compartment of which Ronny opened and, to Tom's surprise, handed him a thin longsword of medieval Norman make. It was polished shiningly, and well-balanced; it was rather heavy, but Tom enjoyed holding it – not that he ever wanted to slash or stab anyone with it. Ronny then led Tom towards the front door, and pointed at a large broken window to the left of the front door, and said, "This is how she got into the house when we were having lunch. I was too excited about the bear to realize that she was missing. So stupid of me!" – he punched himself rather hard in the side of his head, making Tom flinch – "So stupid!"

Then Ronny opened the front door with the key and they went inside; the inside was darker and drearier now that the sun was covered by the rainclouds. There was a certain foreboding to the vestibule this time, a marginalized vacuous silence left over from the soft noise of the rain outside. Tom wanted to see Mother, despite her recent decapitation, mostly to see with his own eyes that it was true. Ronny led the way quietly upstairs (Tom could tell he was frightened) and into the hallway. Tom could hear a muffled, angry ranting voice coming out of Father's room, and he gathered that Father had awakened and Ronny had postponed dealing with him.

"Hey! Is anybody out there? It must be getting on to two o'clock and I need my jar changed! Ronny! Mother!"

Ronny led Tom quietly past Father's room, the door of which had been kicked open and left slightly ajar, and on to Mother's room and, after pausing momentarily at her door and knocking thrice as done habitually, he pushed it open. The blinds were drawn, the room was dark, and only a pale grey glow illuminated the outlines of objects. Tom looked around the room for Mother's body, and his gaze gravitated towards the floor after seeing that she was neither on the bed nor in the armchair. He saw a shape on the floor, and then he saw the dull gleam of a puddle underneath the shape, and then Ronny threw open the blinds of the window to the left and let a flood of weak grey light into the room, illuminating Mother's headless body, lying on its back with its plumpish limbs spread out over the floor, and the pool of blood which was expanding beneath it, but Tom didn't see her head anywhere. Then Ronny opened the other blinds, and Tom turned away and looked out the window at the darkened afternoon. Morbid was the sharp contrast which Tom could not but perceive between the memory of her bouncing, vibrant, breathing body as he had seen it earlier, and the dead, waxy, heavy mass which lay splayed on the floor. He shut his eyes, not wanting to see her head, wishing to go back to his place under the tree.

Ronny put his hand on Tom's left shoulder and said, through heavy gasps, "Her head was damaged irreparably; there is nothing I can do ..." he paused for a moment and sighed loudly, then added, "We are going to need you to perform the T4 on the girl in order to rectify all this, Tom. We were going to have a conception with Mother later on tonight. You are our only hope now."

"I will be only too happy to, Ronny," Tom answered, inwardly realizing that his time of glory had ended and he would have to run away. "I will be only too happy to."

Then Ronny said, "Okay, Tom. It's time to search the house. We'll start with the closet." Ronny looked at Tom expectantly, and Tom realized that Ronny wanted him to search the closet. Apparently Ronny had come into Mother's room, had found her dead, and had fled the house in fear without having searched the rest of it. But he didn't hold it against Ronny, being young and scrawny and probably accustomed to relying upon an experienced hunter, like Jack, perhaps. Fair enough, thought Tom to himself, fair enough.

Tom walked somewhat dejectedly over to the closet and threw it open without hesitation, for he was reasonably certain that he would be able to handle the disheveled girl; the closet was empty except for about five dresses and a couple suits hanging on the bar and a number of boxes piled up along the sides. Tom turned to Ronny in anticipation of further instruction.

"I guess that since the rooms are kept locked, we are left with only Father's room and the room downstairs that she broke into. Let's go!"

They walked out into the hallway and Ronny shut the door behind them, his breath heavy with anxiety and deeply settled panic. Father's voice was hollering out of the room as through a loudspeaker set at very low volume:

"I want food! What the fuck is going on in this place? Where the hell are you, Ronny? Mother! Get over here! I know you are out there, I can hear you! I have a microphone, you know! I need my jar changed and my feed-bottle replenished; I'm starving to death in here!"

Ronny regarded the door to Father's room, slightly ajar, with horror. Tom waited for him to say something, but when Ronny said nothing he walked forward and pushed the door open. As the door swung open, Tom saw that something new was sitting on the desk: a bright white thin plaque-like thing which shone with its own energy, rising out of a similarly sized and similarly shaped low case sitting flat on the desktop, which, judging by its size and colour, Tom could only guess to be the waking state of the great HP.

Ronny gasped as he saw this, and ran over to the desk. "Oh my God!" he hissed, "Oh my God! She woke HP! She saw HP unsupervised! She used almost all of his time!"

Tom came up behind him, wanting to see HP's face more closely. He looked over Ronny's shoulder and saw, silhouetted blackly at the top centre of the glowing white plaque, the words PORTENTUS STOMACHI above a dark dense text, and then Ronny put HP to sleep and the plaque went black.

Ronny looked at Tom, and whispered under Father's bellowing, "Tom, you've never heard of *Portentus Stomachi*, have you?" but, remembering the limited extent of Tom's knowledge, he said, "Oh, never mind." He seemed lost for a moment in his thoughts, momentarily transcending his panic in his pensiveness, and then he returned to the moment and looked uneasily at the closet.

"Ronny! Open this fucking door right now! I command you in the name of the forefathers and the great HP, open this door!"

Ronny seemed to make a decision, and he turned to Tom and said, "Tom, if you would be so good as to search the room, which you will find last door on the left down the hall which goes down left from the vestibule, and if she's not there then look for her outside, and if you find the girl," his face suddenly contracted into a snarl of fierce vengefulness and he hissed, "bring her back to me alive."

Ronny then opened a drawer in the desk and took out a keychain and handed it to Tom, pointing out the key to the front door. Tom left, not wanting to meet Ronny's father when he was in such a foul mood, and went down the hallway, down the stairs, through the vestibule and down the hall to the room as Ronny had instructed. Finding the door similarly kicked open, he looked inside: it was an uninteresting room with no carpet, nothing hanging on the walls, and yellowed sheets covered a couch and two armchairs. There was a stained brown upright piano against the wall to his right, its top half covered by a sheet. There was no-one in the room and no closet in which one might hide. Tom walked back down the hall, out through the vestibule and, unlocking the front door, out onto the front porch. He locked the door behind him, put the keychain into the right forepocket of his jeans, and looked off the porch at the neighbourhood.

- II -
The Chase in the Forest

It was raining heavily, and the houses of the neighbourhood looked different, more frightening and mysterious than they had earlier: from the gashes and holes in the houses seemed to peek hidden creatures, or ghosts. But the grass, the trees that stood between the houses, everything green seemed to drink and soak happily under the pouring rain. Everything seemed to be shifting subtly, half-camouflaged by the hazy movement of the precipitation, and grow and freshen palpably. Tom felt terrific, physically vigorous, charged with productive libidinous energy, the bear meat having done its job excellently. Everything again seemed tuned to a great aquatic pulse, but while earlier he had been subjugated and overpowered by the pulse, powerless in its throes, now he felt like he was master of the pulse. He felt full of superhuman strength and energy, and his mind seemed to add its own extravagant embellishments to the slowly heaving movements of the fauna under the rain, creating a robust liveliness which expanded with a crawling boundlessness under the generous rainstorm.

Tom leapt down the porch stairs, which were wide, and walked down the path towards the road, swinging his longsword about. When he arrived at the side of the road he turned his head up to the sky and opened his mouth to let the drops fall in. They fed his exuberance: his breast expanded like a balloon; he stretched to his full height and inhaled deeply. He reached a climactic pitch of physiological self-affirmation, and then the image of the disheveled girl flashed vividly across his mind. He thought of her dirty face, her scratched bronze skin under her ragged, torn clothing, and he thought that she was probably soaking now under the storm, running away from her determined hunters, the rain washing off the dirt, cleansing her, revealing her. Tom focussed his sight far up into the grey cloudy sky, and he seemed to sense her presence there, in the rain which was falling abundantly and changing her, changing him, changing everything, into something else, something fresher, something wetter.

Tom bade farewell to the house, and impulsively began running up the road, towards the redbrick house which appeared to be the only other house on the block that was intact. He ran spryly, with great agility, skipping over the gravel road like an ostrich or a cheetah, and dove through the hedge which extended around the backyard of the redbrick house, his longsword swiping a slit through the hedge with sharp surgical accuracy. As he emerged on the other side of the hedge, he realized that he had entered a large, forested backyard which spread behind the house to the south and east for miles. The forest sloped downhill, eastwards, into a little valley, the bottom of which he could not see through the trees. Tom couldn't reconcile the immensity or the geography of the forest with his earlier impression of the neighbourhood at all: it seemed far too large to fit into the block, and seemed to take up all of the space which had earlier been occupied by the houses on this block and on the blocks beyond.

Then he heard the voice of a young woman, a voice he had not heard before: "You are looking for me, I suppose?" Tom started, and looked ahead of him, southwards, in the direction from which the voice seemed to have come. A moment later, he heard it from his left, a ticklish whisper in his ear, "I give up: you've found me."

He saw the disheveled girl, no longer dirty, but clean and naked, her slim, lissome sunbronzed body framed between the dripping leaves of the trees, standing on a harsh grey rock about ten feet away. Her face, no longer frowning, no longer weeping, but clean and shiny from the rain; her hair, sleek and flattened around her oval skull, hanging like brown weeds down her goosebumped shoulders; her little white breasts; her arms, scratched but clean, hanging at her sides; her hands, closing over the central vertex amid the width of her hips; her brown eyes fixed blackly on Tom: all surrendered, relinquished.

Tom, perplexed, looked at her, feeling a heaviness gather in his penis, a tightness in his testicles, and said, "Decapitation is quite uncalled for."

Then suddenly she sprang off into the trees with the swiftness and dexterity of a cat, and he heard her voice call back, "I read a story this afternoon, just after lunch. It was called *Portentus Stomachi*. I didn't get to finish it, because I was interrupted by that kid screaming about his dead mum, and I thought I should get out of there."

Tom dropped his longsword and ran after her, leaping with equal dexterity, following her voice, swinging from branch to branch like a monkey, hopping from rock to rock like a cricket, cutting through the leaves like a hawk, skimming along the branches like a squirrel, her taut rear, bronzed legs and small feet gleaming teasingly at times through the foliage. Tom called after her, "Why don't you tell me about it? Good stuff?"

"Pretty good stuff," her high voice called at him through the trees, as she continued to weave her way through the forest, down towards the bottom of the valley. "It has its weak points, but it's not a bad read."

Tom tore off his shirt, as it was impeding him, and said, "Does it have anything to do with Frydish Nitskee? I hear he was a rather complex individual."

"If you mean Friedrich Nietzsche, then yes, it has everything to do with him, and many other people, too." For a second she stopped on a thick bough, long enough for Tom to reach out and swipe his hand down her back, but his hand and her back were wet, and he couldn't get a grip, and she darted off through the trees.

"How about Plato?"

"Him too."

"And Schopenhauer?"

"It has absolutely nothing to do with Schopenhauer."

"Who is the main character?" he asked.

"One character is a fellow called Tom."

"Tom? But that's my name!"

"And the other character is a young woman called Summa."

"Summa? That's a silly name!"

Suddenly Tom was on top of her; she had landed sitting on a huge felled tree-trunk, soggy and mossy, foamy underfoot. Tom only just managed not to fall on her. She looked up at him reproachfully, "But that's my name."

"Oh? I'm so sorry. I've just never known anybody with that name before. What happens in this story?"

"I didn't get very far. I was interrupted by that kid screaming about his dead mother, just when Tom took his pants off," – she pushed him off the trunk, and he pulled down his wet pants robotically – "Summa opened her legs," – still seated, she turned towards him and opened her legs until they formed an M around the slim hourglass of her torso, and she turned her chin up and looked at the trees pensively – "and then – let me think – I think Tom was about to do something, the consequences of which had, earlier in the story, been implied as being rather far-reaching, but I hate stories where the author tries to make you think that something is going to happen without telling you what it is. You know, Tom, I like plain-speaking in a story; I don't go for all this elaborate harbingering. Let things happen when they happen, don't talk about them before they happen! That's not how things happen in real life, is it, Tom?" She turned her eyes down from the sky onto him, her chin still pointed upwards, her oval head slightly aslant. Water flowed in thin and thickening streams down her legs and torso, dripped off onto the moss; she slowly fell backwards onto her elbows, her gaze still fixed on Tom expectantly. "But I didn't get to finish the story, so I guess I'll never know, making it doubly irritating."

Tom's penis had been growing steadily throughout the previous speech, and now it stood full and erect, pointed towards her wet body. His testicles rose and tightened; his muscles twitched; his pulse quickened; and a gushing heat spread throughout his body, firing him from within. He said, "Yes, it is rather unrealistic," and his gaze traveled from her eyes down her body: over her trembling lips, over her shivering neck, shoulders, chest and belly, to her vagina, a black hole of infinite tension and zero density, a singularly enigmatic singularity, and he floated towards it like a sail in a calm but steady wind, aiming to fill it with a brighter mass of infinite tension and considerable density.

As they touched, Tom's vision was overwhelmed by a wave of images. He thought he was traveling through a wormhole at incredible velocity – stars spinning and whizzing by, colours swirling and mixing all around him – which caused intense dizziness, making him feel lightheaded and weak in his knees. Interspersed throughout this vision at regular intervals were other very vivid visions of particular scenes which seemed somehow external to him, unfamiliar, as opposed to the visions he had had a little earlier while digesting the bear meat under the tree in the backyard which had all been familiar.

Soon Tom was not at all aware of the sensations he was experiencing in the strange forest with the wet girl at all; he was completely disembodied and hallucinating.

He was first flying through a wormhole, as explained above: colours of every kind swirled and spread and vanished and merged and created beautiful and complex designs all around him; stars whizzed by at incredible speed; the wormhole took him up and down and left and right and in every other direction unpredictably at what felt like an ultimate velocity (the speed of light, no doubt, but this did not occur to Tom) and very smoothly. Then suddenly he landed on a slim tower which overlooked from great height a large sprawling seaside city. He smelt the salt in the air, and felt the wind in his hair, and he was leaning forward over the railings facing towards the ocean a few kilometres ahead of him. The sun was hanging, plummeting downwards slowly before him, and Tom thought it must be the middle of the afternoon. He looked down and saw that the tower was standing in the middle of a large wide street which stretched to the left and right, and gazing rightwards he saw it turn into a bridge which stretched over a thin river some distance to the south. The street was filled with cars of an early twentieth-century style, and trams moved up and down the middle of the road. The city was regular in a somewhat irregular way; the buildings often looked different in colour and slightly different in style, but they were similar in size and layout, and most were simple rectangular blocks containing about sixteen windows in their sides, and most were three stories tall. Then he saw two middle-aged women standing to the right of him, both leaning over the railing of the tower and looking off in a kind of silent wonder. They were both dressed similarly, both wearing brightcoloured skirts, light summer jackets and bonnets. There were two black umbrellas of slightly different length leaned up against a wide circular stone pillar which took up most of the tower-top; Tom looked up and saw, straining his neck, that there was a statue at the top of this pillar about ten feet up, an important-looking officer wearing a large tricorn and holding his sword with his left hand at his waist in swashbuckling fashion; he appeared to be missing his right arm. The two women did not seem to be interested in or even aware of Tom; they both gazed silently out at the view, the wind making their skirts flap against their age-widened bodies. Tom thought that they were middle-aged because of their wrinkled faces peering out from their bonnets and the worn texture of their legs beneath their skirts, their varicose veins. They were excited and seemed to be holding their breath and gasping at intervals, but both their brows were similarly knit in an expression at once sad and awestruck, as though they both felt that they were realizing something beautiful too late, and this lent a particular tinge of conscious deprivation to their faces. Then Tom heard, very loudly, a young man's voice. The voice was not too deep, a youthful tenor which spoke confidently and even a little haughtily, and which sounded moreover like the speaker knew more than he was saying, or like he was trying to say something indirectly, cleverly. Tom knew from the tone that the young man was talking to an audience of at least a few people by the way that he articulated the words precisely, like a practiced orator. The voice said: "But they are afraid the pillar will fall. They see the roofs and argue about where the different churches are ..." But Tom did not get to hear the young man finish his sentence, for he was snatched up once more into the wormhole and transported, over wide seas and fields and forests and hills and farms and towns and cities and mountains, and then more seas, and then more fields and mountains and things, until he was brought to another city, this one further inland, and deposited in a small room where a man was sitting at a desk under a window, dressed in a wrinkled white shirt, his head supported by his left hand, supported in turn by his elbow on the desk, squinting at some papers on the table. He had a moustache and a small beard which was confined to the area of his chin and left his cheeks cleanshaven. He wore small round glasses with very thick lenses. His brown hair was oiled darkly against his scalp, but it was ruffled on the left side of his scalp where he had been scratching and rubbing it with his left fingers in pensive agitation. The man looked like he was involved in extremely deep thought, or puzzlement, or frustration, and then all of a sudden the man brought his left arm down on the table with a woody bang and cursed: "Blast!" Then Tom was snatched up once more by the wormhole, and this time he was brought back into outer space for a while and shot around at tremendous velocity, witnessing many beautiful bright intergalactic phenomena. His whole body shivered spasmodically in the throes of an ecstatic vibration which emanated from his stomach and spread outwards throughout his limbs – a kind of giddy, bubbling warmth in his belly and loins, contorting the muscles of his face into a grin and pulling him back by the shoulders as though he were on a rollercoaster. There were red and green lights snaking and dancing around in elaborately beautiful shapes and designs, mirroring the warm glow in his body. Tom was completely captivated by the sounds, the feelings, the sights, and, most of all, by how they all seemed to coalesce in a single feeling of rippling, twinkling bliss. He felt like such entertainment could never grow tedious; indeed, it seemed to him to be a kind of purified entertainment, having magically done away with the exhaustible middle-man means. The shapes and designs swirled and danced around in his vision, like smoke, like waves, and there was a peculiar pixelized quality to them, like the whole vision was made up of millions of stars. Sometimes he saw familiar shapes: steamboats on water; a highway stretching into the distance; female eyes; lit windows; cars; aeroplanes; letters and numbers and more letters in different languages, runes and hieroglyphics and ancient symbols. The vision seemed to be thickening and condensing very slowly, and his vision became redder and greener, the pixels piling on top of each other like snowflakes, until a kind of maximum density was reached and the most extraordinary thing happened: the whole thing blew up and shattered into its billion parts, and spread out at a supreme speed in every direction. As the explosion occurred, Tom felt like his mind was exploding too, emptying. It was like witnessing the big bang, a metaphysical firework sweeping his mind with a vertiginous wave making him stagger and nearly fall down. All of the pixels scattered and disappeared at once, and he was left with void, yawning and sucking him into outer reaches of infinity. Then, a few moments later, a little red dot appeared in the centre of his vision, followed shortly by two beams of light, stretching horizontally and vertically, intersecting at the red dot like a Cartesian graph, and then this cross was crossed by two more beams which also intersected at the red dot, forming an X over the cross and together forming a star. Then other red and green dots joined the original dot at this central vertex, and the same swirling and spinning images began building upon this base until his vision began filling up again with the images. He felt the pressure build up in his head, more keenly aware this time, and he didn't breathe at all while the beautiful images condensed and spun and danced once more, so heartstoppingly beautiful they were, and they built up and spread out and elaborated until the vision began reaching its maximum density again, and Tom could feel it coming, and he braced himself, and then all of a sudden the whole thing blew up again, and Tom inhaled sharply, flabbergasted, his heart skipped several beats, and he almost fell back onto the ground. But then Tom was wrenched away and shot again into the wormhole, and he landed, after many moments of flying through space at the speed of light, back where he had started, in the wet rainy forest, only now it was shrunken down to a normal-sized overgrown backyard, one which could easily fit into the space it had previously occupied.

The rain had mostly stopped, leaving only a light drizzle. Much to Tom's chagrin, the sex was finished. Summa was collecting her garments, no longer the tattered rags in which they had found her by the stream, but rather a pair of jeans and a white T-shirt with which the family had presumably furnished her. She was shivering from the rain, and looked worried. Tom had a feeling of hazy, grateful riddance, and his penis ached. His head was filled with a warm, happy fuzz, and a glimmering afterglow of dopamine lent its sheen to the dark sparkle of the wet leaves and drizzling rain. He no longer felt capable of superhuman feats, and his body felt heavy and his muscles lazed, and he was somewhat dubious as to what would happen next; he thought that they would have to run away, and realized fearfully that escape would not be easy considering the number and determination of the hunters, and also how close they were to the house.

Then, right on cue, Tom heard voices through the hedge, and he knew that it would only be a matter of time before an armed teen or two would come into the yard in search of the girl. Tom hastily pulled his pants back on, threw on his shirt, and picked up the longsword which lay a few paces away in the weeds by the hedge. Tom considered going out through the hedge and announcing to the hunters that there was no-one here, and he looked at Summa, who was now dressed and rubbing her arms with their opposite hands in an effort to get warm and looking at him with a measure of uncertainty. Tom tried to look self-assured, and said, "I am going to tell these kids to go away; I will be back in a jiffy."

He crawled his way through the hedge back the way he had come, much less nimbly and with considerable difficulty, feeling more sluggish with every move, his clothes snagged by the twigs, the water dripping coldly on his back, and emerged back into the street a jumbled mess of tripping limbs. He saw a group of three young people down the road to the east, two boys and a girl, all dressed in the common white T-shirt and faded blue jeans and brandishing hatchets or butchers' knives, who looked up at him as he emerged. They seemed surprised, and the deference in their faces reminded Tom that he was the Solstice Hero. They hesitated and almost bumped into each other, an obvious sign of their fear of him, and this further increased Tom's confidence.

Before he could even get a clear view of their faces he said with a serious assertive tone (by now he was well-practiced), "She's not in these few yards over here," gesturing back at the hedge. "I'll check inside the redbrick house and the one next to it, and you guys go and check in those yards up there," he added, pointing behind him up the street to the west.

The three nodded obediently and lowered their heads deferentially and continued the way they were coming, giving Tom a wide berth as they passed, up towards the next block which lay above the road, called Meade, which turned left off their road after the redbrick one in whose backyard stood, or sat, the girl. Tom looked around the street. The rain had stopped, stripping the atmosphere of the magical interconnecting aquatic film which had created such robust movement and liveliness, leaving everything wet but bounded, grounded, the air dry and empty, no longer an easy passage for ambitious faunal expansion. The unseen ghosts of the houses retreated back into their dark soggy rooms, and a few visible creatures poked their heads out tentatively. The grey clouds were rolling over, still speedily, leaving in their wake the glow of lighter clouds. Looking west, Tom saw clear blue sky beyond the wave of whiteness, and thought there would probably be a rainbow soon. Before long the sun peeked through cracks in the white clouds, covering Tom in a warming waft of brightness. It made him feel sluggish and thirsty.

Tom looked around a little, noting a few hunters' heads over the hedge at the end of the yard behind the house across the street and hearing talking from down the road, and then he turned around and prepared to reenter the hole in the hedge, but noticed that by the redbrick wall of the house the hedge left a space wide enough for him to slip through with less difficulty; he strolled over and reentered the back yard this easier way. The girl was still there, shivering in the shade of the house. Tom thought it would be best to run southwards, through the block, their chances of being seen in the street behind being too high. But in fact he was quite certain that they would be caught.

There was only one row of houses stretching eastwards down the other side of the block before the next street southwards, the block being a typical two-by-two stretching from Meade street in the west eastwards towards the bottom of the valley. Tom took the girl's hand (she said nothing), and they walked slowly, Tom with great trepidation, wading silently through the tall grass towards the next street. Tom prickled at the sound of voices from the street behind them, youthful energetic voices, "Those houses are clear!" and "You guys go that way!" Tom for some reason wondered how Ronny was faring with his wrathful father.

They both squeezed through the hedge dividing the redbrick house's yard from the next one, and then Tom led Summa as lightly and quietly as he could through the yard behind the next house, this one white, towards a wide opening between two trees which stood in the yard to the south of the house, beyond which lay the next road. Reaching the side of the tree on the right, Tom told Summa to wait quietly while he made sure the coast was clear. He walked out over the six feet of yard and onto the sidewalk, looking around, and didn't see anybody or hear anything anywhere. He paused for a moment on the sidewalk; the sun was out now, and looking up he saw a wide rainbow stretching down into the land to the south from high above behind him in the northern sky. Bursting, lushly oozing was the fresh greenness of the happy benefiters of the high summer rain.

He gestured for Summa to follow him, and she came out into the road. Then he heard, making his heart skip a beat in fright, the creak and clatter of the carriage's wheels from the left as it pulled up the road from the east. He looked down, and saw the carriage tearing up the road quickly, the two horses looking even bigger and more muscular than they had earlier – more bear meat magic, no doubt. He saw them just as Summa got to his side, and he grabbed her left forearm and said, "Don't worry! I can talk us out of this. We'll escape later. Don't say a word: be mute like you were before!"

Summa, her thin wrist still, said nothing. Tom was not sure that he would be able to help her, but he selfishly wanted to reassure her to make it all easier for him. Deep down, Tom felt that if Summa did not want to be hunted, she should not have decapitated Mother and abused HP. If she could not escape on her own, why should it be his job to help her? And if she had not wanted to have sex with him, she should have kept her clothes on. He considered for a moment why he was in this situation, and realized that the main reason he was helping her was a certain abject sense of obligation resultant of their recent copulation; it seemed at best awkward and at worst cruel to simply abandon her after so recently having had sex with her. But he himself was guilty only of lying about his true abilities, out of simple fear, and of having given in to his lust after having been provoked while possessed by bear meat. He wondered, shooting her an sharp side-glance, whether he even liked her at all, apart from his sexual attraction to her, and decided that he had no reason to. Why should he involve himself in the self-inflicted troubles of Summa? Whatever would happen could not be worse than either an earthquake or an encounter with Donald Murchader – of this he was quite certain. He decided that he would not endanger himself for her sake, her crimes being her own, but he would try to keep her out of harm's way (insofar as it posed no danger to himself); after all, he was the Solstice Hero and he could do whatever he wanted, could he not? All this he thought as the carriage came swiftly up the road and George and Jack leapt down off the driver's seat like a flash. In a moment they were standing before Tom and Summa, their brawny arms crossed victoriously over their diaphragms. George said, "Good job, Tom!"

Tom smiled and said, "Thank you, but it was nothing."

George and Jack stood grinning admiringly at Tom for a while, and then George said, "Let's bring her to Ronny."

"Okay."

Tom brought Summa into the passenger booth and George and Jack returned to the driver's seat. Summa stared out the window, inscrutably indifferent, during the whole ride. Beneath the surface of dubiousness, Tom could not help but feel accomplished.

- 12 -
Ronny's Plan

The ride around the block took no time at all. When they arrived back at the house, Tom heard George's voice calling, "We've got her! Everybody return to camp!"

The right door to the carriage swung open and Jack's handsome face said, "I'll tell Ronny you've found her; can I have the keys?" Tom, having forgotten about the keys, searched his pockets and pulled a heavy keychain out of his right pocket and threw it at Jack; Jack caught the keys and disappeared.

Tom said, half to himself, "Don't worry: I am the Solstice Hero," and Summa rolled her eyes.

They both clambered out of the carriage, and a crowd of armed youths began gathering around the two. Their faces seemed blank, or perhaps Tom had stopped looking at them. In a moment the front door of the house opened and shut and Ronny and Jack came hurrying down to the driveway and Ronny said, "Good job Tom! I don't know what we'd do without you."

Tom shrugged and said, "It is my pleasure, Ronny. I told you you would not regret your decision."

Ronny's face broke into a smile of relief, in which the whole crowd basked for a time; it was the first time Ronny's moroseness had lifted since the discovery of Mother's decapitation. Then, after a long moment, Ronny said, "Well, do your thing."

Tom realized with sinking heart that Ronny was referring to the T4 technique, and they wanted him to do it to the girl to undo her killing of Mother, her reading of HP, and many more things. But luckily for him, he had a plan. After inhaling deeply, Tom said in his most assertive voice, "I am afraid, Ronny, that that is out of the question."

Ronny's smile of relief lingered for a moment while the brightness was drained out of his eyes and replaced by dull perplexity. Then he blinked and said, "Why?"

"Well, Ronny, you see, my Father told me never to T4 a lady. This is one of the oaths I took before learning the technique."

Ronny began breathing heavily; his upper lip twitched; he blinked in somewhat neurotic fashion; finally he said, "What? How can that be? She's not a lady! She's an evil, evil girl ... she killed Mother!" Ronny began trembling and looked like he was going to start crying, and Tom knew that he had won.

"All that aside, Ronny, my friend, it was an oath and we ... Toms take our oaths seriously. Consider that the master of the T4 technique must have a clear conscience and a clean soul, and this is where our superhuman strength comes from! No, such strength is not endowed naturally, but supernaturally, as the result of spiritual fortitude and impeccable moral character! Ronny, surely you must understand this after all that you have read!" Tom tossed his longsword into the grass by the driveway and came forward and put his right hand on Ronny's shaking shoulder, "Surely you must know that!"

Ronny brought his right hand up to his brow and began sobbing, but his head was nodding in agreement, "Yes, Tom, I know."

"Even if I wanted to, the inherent wrongness of the proposed act would rob me of the strength needed to do it. She has done wrong, I know. But she is somebody's daughter, somebody's sister, perhaps – I don't think she's a mother, but someday she may be – and I cannot do what you ask. Be merciful, Ronny. Some things cannot be undone, must not be undone, and we must build anew upon the possibilities that are left to us."

Ronny nodded and began regaining his composure. His sobbing ceased, and his hand moved to the top of his head where it began scratching in familiar token that he was beginning to think proactively again. Tom removed his hand from his shoulder, and the whole crowd, which had now grown to about twenty people or more, stood quietly and stared at Ronny, waiting to see what he would do. Ronny's brow furrowed, his eyes squinted at the gravel of the driveway, and his hand moved down to his chin which it began stroking in the customary fashion. After a long time of thinking, he looked up at Tom and said, "The thing is, Tom, we were going to have a conception with Mother tonight, for the Autumn Equinox."

Tom, marveling at the quick passing of the seasons, said, "Is that so?"

Ronny nodded, "Yes, Tom, that is so. But I have a plan. The only way that we can still go on with it is to replace Mother with another woman."

This statement struck Tom as a strange one, and he repeated, "Replace Mother with another woman?"

"Yes. You see, Mother was not really a mother yet. She was going to become one, after conception. Mother is chosen by Father during Spring Equinox, kept in top condition throughout summer, and then we have a conception." He put an emphasis on every noun in that sentence, as though he was talking to a four-year-old, then added, "That is how we have done things since time immemorial, as set down by the forefathers."

"Of course," said Tom, "that makes perfect sense."

Then Ronny sharpened in the manner which Tom had come to recognize as indicative of his getting a good idea and said, "Now if you will excuse me, I have just had a brilliant idea. I need to do some reading while there is still time. Jack! I need your help: come with me inside to confer with Father." The two departed and left Tom and Summa with the crowd of youths.

The crowd stood silently for a time, and Tom began feeling somewhat awkward with so many eyes upon him: everybody in the group was studying him and Summa, causing him to feel quite uncomfortable, paranoid that the youths could somehow perceive that he and Summa had recently had sex. He looked at George, George being the only one in the group he recognized, and noticed that George's eyes were fixed upon Summa, a look of outrage slowly taking over his sunny features. Then suddenly George pointed at her and cried, "She's been seeded!"

The whole crowd gasped in unison, and Tom looked at Summa and noticed, to his great surprise, a noticeable bulge in her stomach, about the the size of a softball, only just apparent beneath her loose T-shirt, which had not been there the last time he had looked at her. The crowd began speaking and arguing and whispering in astonishment, "It's true!" "Look at that!" and "Oh my."

Tom looked closely at Summa's bulging stomach, certain that it had not been thus twenty minutes hence when he had seen her naked in the backyard of the redbrick house. She covered the bulge self-consciously with her right hand and looked questioningly at Tom; Tom thought he saw the bulge move beneath her fingers, and he met her gaze and shrugged as if to say, "I don't know."

After a few moments George asked Tom, "What state was she in when you caught her?"

Tom replied, "The state of running away."

George brought his right hand up to his heavy chin and looked down at the gravel in Ronnyesque fashion and mused silently for a few moments; finally he said, "Well, this is not good, not good at all. We must inform Ronny; but meanwhile, lock her up in the shed." The crowd murmured assent, and George took Summa by the arm and they all headed towards the backyard of the house.

Tom did not know exactly how he felt about the situation. He didn't feel like the bulge in her stomach had anything to do with him –

rather, the possibility that the astonishingly, even horrifically quickly growing bulge in her belly was *his* offspring was absolutely far too insane for him to take seriously, or to even remotely occur to him. He thought rather, if he thought of it at all (for he was getting used to ignoring things which made too little sense to him), that something else, something completely unrelated to him, was responsible for the bulge in her stomach – indigestion, some frightening tropical disease, a rare type of extreme cancer, or extra-terrestrials, for instance. The bulge changed things: he was losing his sense of obligation to the girl, feeling both detached from and too uncomfortably close to her situation, and although he felt sorry for her and still hoped to help her escape later if he could, he was increasingly wanting to distance himself from her as much as possible in the eyes of the youths. Things had turned out all right for him: his position as Solstice Hero was not threatened, and his bluff had worked well; no-one doubted him; if anything his position was even more powerful than before, and he did not want to compromise this by overtly helping Summa. Conflicted, he followed, feeling perhaps a little thirsty, as the group moved to the back yard, the youths talking amongst themselves in hushed whispers.

Suddenly he felt a familiar presence by his right side, and he heard the voice of Calpurnia, "How has your afternoon been, Tom?"

Tom was glad to hear Calpurnia's voice, as he thought of her as his friend, and he answered, "It has been good; I can't complain. A little strange, perhaps, but on the whole I can't complain."

"I am glad to hear that. Mine was boring. It's too bad about Mother."

Tom nodded, "Yes, too bad about Mother."

"I bet he's up to something, though; I bet he'll figure something out; I'm not sure if it'll be something good, but I'm sure he's up to something. He has read too much of the wrong stuff."

"Ronny, you mean. Well, in fact, he did say that he had a brilliant idea."

"Oh no, not a brilliant idea! This is never good." Calpurnia seemed genuinely put off by the thought of Ronny having what he would describe as a brilliant idea, causing Tom to wonder, just a little, what kind of idea was likely to be conceived in Ronny's bespectacled black-tufted well-scratched skull; but this just a little, as he knew well by now that in this world the reality would always be weirder than anything his own nondescript skull was capable of conceiving.

The group stopped moving outside the shed which was located beside a hedge that separated their yard from the yard of the next house to the east; some dispersed in different directions, having lost interest or gotten hungry. Tom watched as George ushered Summa into the shed and shut the door and pulled out a heavy keychain and with a small key thereon locked a padlock on the door and then turned back to the group with a look of serious denouement and said, "That's all for now."

Part Three

- 13 -
Berry-Picking

George began walking officiously towards the house as though he had something important to do (inform Ronny of Summa's impregnation, probably), twirling the keychain around on his right forefinger and whistling aloofly, seeming rather calm and unperturbed by the whole situation. Many youths, however, were not equally aloof, and they continued in their hushed murmurs and emphatic whispers after George had disappeared around the side of the house. Some youths went up to a small window on the shed to the right of the padlocked door, crushing a path through a small weedy garden beneath it, and pushed their faces up to the glass and looked in, saying, "Let me look in!" and "Do you see her?" Tom turned away from the shed, trying not to think of Summa in there alone in her mysterious condition, gawked at by the youths; he still thought rationally that her troubles were of her own making, but he could not deny the clinging feeling that by having had sex with her he had partaken irreversibly of her being, of her fate, in some elusive way which was by him not comprehended, yet.

He looked around for some water and saw a large bucket of it by the extinguished bonfire in the middle of the yard; he went over and picked up a nearby mug, dipped it in, pulled it out and drank; he emptied the mug, and then went in for a second mugfull, and finished that one as well. The water was well-received by his stomach. Then he stood, refreshed, and looked around at the yard: the yard was large and filled with wooden-bordered pentagonal and hexagonal gardens, all of which were overgrown by drooping spurts of unruly weeds; there was a large tree in the corner of the yard up near the house on the side of the driveway, and there was a smaller tree nearer the back of the yard under which he had lain earlier while digesting the bear meat; the whole yard was surrounded by a ten-foot-tall hedge, creating an arena-like aspect, and there was a man-sized hole in the northeast corner of the hedge which led to the yard to the east.

He still felt rather sluggish and tired, and thought he could probably have a snooze somewhere; the digestion of the ample heavy bear meat and the bout of fornication which had soon followed had left him with very little energy. The sun, rich in late summer, threw its yellowing beams over everything, spending, tiring, tiring with its spending. He couldn't think of anything he wanted to do, anything that needed doing, and wondered if there was even anything to do if he wanted to do something. The unrecognized occupations of the youths, involving unidentifiable objects, appeared to be undertaken with a common attitude of having nothing better to do, and seemed on that account rather feckless, and Tom did not feel in the least inclined to join any of them in their mysterious endeavours. Calpurnia was taking some water from the bucket, and Tom began to understand her characteristic bored, rebellious demeanour.

"Is there anything to do around here, Calpurnia?" Tom asked, wanting distraction from his thoughts.

Calpurnia finished off her mug of water and stood and rolled her eyes at the sky and yawned, "Tom, is there ever anything to do anywhere? The gardener tends his garden; the soldier fights his war; the explorer finds his places; the thinker thinks his thoughts; the labourer performs his tasks perhaps wishing the day would end; the pilot flies his Cessna into the sunset chasing the day he doesn't want to end; the dog chews its bone; the lioness runs into the woods with her lion: if you don't know what to do that's your fault."

Tom looked around, thinking it was best to sleep; but he asked, "Do you have any ideas?"

"Pick berries for the feast? There's a raspberry bush up the street beside the redbrick house, and a blackberry bush on the next block."

"Hmm," said Tom, wishing he had not asked the question but had rather lain down somewhere to take a short nap before the feast: berry-picking struck him as a boring procedure, and he wanted to avoid the site of his recent adventure in the backyard of the redbrick house; furthermore, he wanted to sleep away the persistent memory of Summa. The recent incidents had created a mysterious feeling of wrongness, a wrongness camouflaged among the preceding events, not apprehended by his intellect but rather unavoidably intuited by his subconscious. His mind recoiled from the thought of Summa, the wrongness and the inability to comprehend the wrongness. "You know, Calpurnia, I think I'd rather take a nap somewhere for a little while."

"What are you, an old man?" Calpurnia sneered, and Tom looked at her tiredly; she was grimacing at him mockingly.

"I don't know, really; do I look like an old man to you?"

Calpurnia made a show of studying his face closely for a number of seconds; then she said, "Not old enough to need a nap after lunch; but who knows these days." She turned from him dismissively and began strolling hastily towards the road, off to pick berries. Tom, galvanized somewhat into wakefulness by Calpurnia's mocking manner, thought that maybe it was not such a bad idea to pick berries with her after all: he thought that, since she was going there anyway, it might be better if he went to make sure that nothing bad happened, and perhaps there was also something in her tone which suggested that the proposed activity would somehow prove more interesting than he had initially imagined, or maybe there was something else entirely, but at any rate he jogged after her (for she was quick) and said, "Oh well, I guess berry-picking sounds okay."

"Okay," she replied.

They walked across the garden-riddled yard, to the side of the house, Calpurnia picking up a bucket by the hedge on the way, and down the driveway, and then they began walking up the road towards the redbrick house. Tom squinted up at the sun, and thought that it was probably around three o'clock in the afternoon, but this was based on intuition rather than on any experience in the art of time estimation. It was certainly late summer: the embryonic melancholia of that season was spreading tangibly in the faraway air, rising skyward like the light dry pollen, ever so slowly behind the hot joy of the July sky, stirring softly in the distance between their feet and the hidden horizon, moving Tom's breast with a little gasp of awe at the deep tragic beauty, the vast inescapable heartrending splendour of high summer plummeting headfirst into the cool lap of autumn like a bright proud eagle into a shadowed canyon.

They walked up the road towards the redbrick house, Calpurnia's feet clapping in her oversized sandals as she skipped along without a care. Tom followed sluggishly, feeling spent and lazy under the heavy summer sun, his hands in his jeans' forepockets. As they approached the redbrick house, Tom tried to remember if there was anything incriminating in the backyard which might reveal his recent relations with Summa to the clever Calpurnia. He could not remember anything; there was probably nothing; and anyway, Calpurnia was probably too young to think about such things. All the same, however, Tom wanted to avoid going into the backyard of the redbrick house as much as possible.

Much to Tom's relief, Calpurnia led him around the front of the house, which faced westward towards the southbound road called Meade, the house being officially on Meade street, and then she led him across the overgrown front yard, under the large round heads of four thick-trunked trees, then over a white-gravel driveway at the south end of the house, and then she stopped before a large raspberry bush just at the end of the driveway between the house and the southern hedge, Tom feeling comfortably far away from the site, and dropped her bucket in the grass and began picking berries. The bush was full of large raspberries, and Tom went over to the east side of the bush, opposite Calpurnia in the direction of the backyard, and began picking berries.

After filling his left palm with berries, he chose a big healthy-looking dark red one and ate it: it was sweet and juicy, perfectly ripe; it rejuvenated him, and he ate several more berries until he felt fairly satisfied. The berries seemed to create a slight hum of tension in his stomach such as he had experienced earlier on the riverbank, only it was far tamer and not even remotely comparable to the earlier hum in terms of intensity, buffered by bear meat and temporarily relieved of lustihead. Rather, the berries gave him enough energy to engage more actively in the current occupation, and as this occupation was easy his mind was left free to wander for a time as he collected handfuls and dumped them softly into the slowly filling bucket.

Wander his mind did, and before long Tom decided that he was glad he had chosen to go with Calpurnia to pick berries. He found the berry-picking to be a very relaxing, meditative activity. The lowering sun cast its rays in splotches through the leaves of a tall tree which stood between them and Meade street to the west, and there a was a light breeze, together creating an ideal temperature for the undemanding work. Tom felt his strength returning slowly in the wake of the gradually dissipating post-coital afterglow, and he thought that before too long he could eat a proper meal. Subconsciously subduing it with the lax promise that things would turn out all right for Summa, his clinging feeling of wrongness gradually wore off completely along with the afterglow, until he began thinking excitedly, elatedly again, and then before long it was true unequivocally that he was feeling good. He kept on picking berries, the bush's stock seemingly inexhaustible, dropping them softly into the bucket, which seemed unfillable. Yes, he thought to himself, I feel great. He felt energetic, but it was a controllable energy, founded firmly upon well-digested bear meat, green vegetables, water and a handful of raspberries, not as restless and aggressive as the energy he had felt in the morning when hunting the bear on a recently-emptied stomach, nor either nearly as frenetic and tense as that which he had experienced after drinking the riverwater, nor yet again as superpowerfully libidinous as that by which he had been possessed while chasing Summa through the magical forest; rather, it was a kind of energetic equilibrium – his mind, his body, his whole being and all its composite parts needed nothing from anything nor from one another; they seemed to balance each other perfectly, leaving nothing but the pure piercing clarity of his thought, unfettered and unneedy, free to do as it willed, to occupy positions as it wished, to be whatever it desired, its bodily extension waiting obediently for its commands. The quality of his thought was elegantly wholesome: every thought, no matter how inconsequential, seemed to soar on its own wind, feed on its own inspiration, encouraged and strong, his heart a well-proved powerhouse: fields of flowers; apple-trees; crisp late summer afternoon canoeing on a still northern lake, swans taking off over the pines; an old-world castle-town in the mountains, snowy peaks reflected shiningly in the huge clean windows. Ronny, George, Jack, the kids, Summa, Father, Mother, were all a joke; that world had gone wrong somewhere; it had been misled; it was mistaken – *this* was all that was real: the awesome churning of the immaculately crafted chambers of his heart. He felt masterful, controlled; he looked forward to the feast, eager to further enjoy his position of easy power over the fresh faceless youths, admiring gullible youths, his loins twitching lustfully at the thought of imposing his will, whatever it may be.

After they had been picking berries for about forty-five minutes, when the bucket was about three-quarters full of big red raspberries, Calpurnia looked up at Tom from across the bush and said, "Do you want to see something interesting before we head back to the house?"

Tom, up for just about anything, said, "Sure, Calpurnia, why don't you show me something interesting?"

Bringing her little right forefinger up to her lips she whispered softly, "Shh; it's a secret!" and she led Tom to a window a few paces away from the raspberry bush in the south side of the redbrick house. Looking around first, she pulled the wooden-paned window upwards and reached with her hand into the room and pulled a short thick plank out from beneath the window and propped the window a foot open therewith. Then she gestured at Tom to go in through the window, bringing her right forefinger up to her lips again urging quiet. Tom, now somewhat dubious, stuck his head and shoulders through the open window into the room: it smelled a little musty, but it seemed tidy and much less rotten than he imagined the other houses in the neighbourhood to be; it was even in good condition – just lacking fresh air. Pushing with his hands on the sill, he brought his body slowly into the room, having difficulty at the point when his crotch reached the sill, then after overcoming this somehow with some pain and discomfort feeling Calpurnia kick him in his flailing foot as he fell inside with a carpet-muffled bang. A moment later Calpurnia was in after him, and she took the plank out from the window and put it back in its place under the sill and let the window down, all without a sound.

Tom sat up and looked around the room: it was surprisingly clean, lacking the stifled spiderweb-ridden atmosphere he had expected. It was a living room, carpeted and fully furnished with two armchairs, a couch, a coffee table in the middle, a small table with a lamp against the far north wall between the two armchairs, a closet in the east wall to his right next to the couch, a bookshelf against the west wall, another window in the west wall and a door in the north wall, and a black upright piano to his left against the south wall through which they had entered. A painting of a bale of hay in a yellow field with a white lighthouse standing in the background hung on the north wall, and a red quilt hung on the east wall. Sunlight fell warmly through the west window onto the thick grey carpet and part of the coffee table. The room seemed very out of place, hidden quietly amid the dilapidated thrown-together and falling apart world outside; it reminded him somewhat of the castle in which he had found himself that morning, but the room seemed very far away from the castle, and the morning seemed like a long time ago. And, moreover, while the castle had felt like it was inhabited by a very kind and gentle absent host, this house was undeniably abandoned, even eerily, for there was no doubt in Tom's mind that whoever had lived here as it was at this moment was now long dead. Eery also was the remarkable feeling that he was being watched, not by a cat, but by a ghost, which feeling made Tom have second thoughts about coming into the house; he felt an unignorable presence, an invisible mass of dark matter, an otherworldly gaze fixed fast upon him.

Without a word Calpurnia went over to the piano bench, opened it, and began looking inside and rustling the papers therein. Tom rose to his feet and stepped quietly two paces to the coffee table hoping to find clues about the house's erstwhile occupier from the books on the table. He saw a pile of magazines stacked vertically, the top one entitled NATIONAL GEOGRAPHIC with a sharp picture of a blue and green planet in space (Earth). Looking down at the lower right corner of the cover-page, Tom saw a name written in tall type above an address, but Tom could not read the name or the address, try as he might; his eyes refused to focus on the letters, myopically missing them, blurring them; he tried backing up, moving closer and to the left and right, but he absolutely could not read the name no matter what vantage point he took. Tom thought the name was familiar somehow, despite his not being able to read it, but there was again a blank spot in his memory, so he forgot about it and went towards the wooden door in the north wall, which was open ajar, and pulled it gently open just as Calpurnia began playing a few soft notes on the piano, a facile thing: triads moving slowly up the predictable whole- and half-tones of the unaltered major scale until the fourth was reached, then dropping back down a third, then going back up again four degrees and dropping three, repeating, and so on, moving thus up the tonal spectrum until the octave was reached, and then beginning all over again. Amazingly, the piano was perfectly in tune.

Tom walked out into the hallway and looked around. Before him there was a carpeted staircase leading eastwards upstairs, a parallel hallway to his right leading eastwards, also carpeted, a closed door across from him, and the large wooden front door of the house to his left. The hallway had cream-coloured wallpaper, yellowed in many places, splotched with little flowers not large enough to be tacky but delicate and slender of petal. He hesitated for some time in the doorway, as he was nervous, wary of the powerful presence he sensed, now more strongly, in the house, but he was also possessed by an intense curiosity, an urge to learn more, if possible, about the house's owner. Finally his curiosity got the better of him: he considered going down the hallway, but decided not to because he expected the kitchen to lie in that direction, and he didn't want to see the kitchen, so he chose to explore upstairs instead, just as Calpurnia started playing what sounded like a real song, as opposed to the previous mindless chord merry-go-round, in the same major key; the song was upbeat, quick, but not moronically happy as is the danger with songs of such description – there was a certain Teutonic sophistication and seriousness to it (of course Tom did not think of it in these terms, but the effect was the same for him as for anyone), and Tom was surprised that Calpurnia could play so well.

He began walking slowly up the stairs, with much trepidation as he was frightened of the house and of what he might find upstairs, feeling his shoes sink into the thick dusty carpet, running his left fingers along the bumpy flowery wallpaper and dragging his right hand loosely along the dark well-worn wooden railing. The place was musty, but not excessively and uncleanly so – the air one might expect to find in an old well-insulated house which still has people living in it – causing Tom to wonder if someone, Calpurnia perhaps, took care of the house, dusting it and keeping the spiders at bay. But all this also increased the eery haunted feeling of the place, and Tom suddenly felt afraid and stopped a moment and looked back down the stairs nervously to make sure nobody was sneaking up behind him. There was nothing there, and the music, now more complicated, was tapping steadily out from the living room.

Tom turned forward again and looked up the stairs: there was a small two-by-two-foot window in the wall directly opposite the head of the stairs opening eastwards, through which he could see the clear blue late summer afternoon sky. He wanted to look out this window, and the urge to do so grew quickly within him, until he was soon atwitter with the desire to go up there and look out the window, held back only by his fear of the eery presence in the house, now stronger than ever. He deliberated laboriously for a while over the question, and then the decision was made for him and his legs started carrying him upwards towards the blue sky beyond the window, his fear increasing, his skin prickling, his hairs standing up on end, his ears cowering as he floated up the stairs, half against his will, like a sail possessed by a calm but steady wind. The climb seemed to take a long time, the staircase stretching out far before him, and the ten remaining steps felt like fifty. When he finally arrived at the top of the stairs he rested his arms on the sill, and looked out the window.

The sun, well out of sight behind him in the western sky, was setting at full tilt, diving towards the horizon; there was no more than a few hours of sunlight left; autumn was lurking ahead, its arms open ready for summer's sleepy head. Tom could see the sparkling shingles of the roof of the house next door, and far beyond it lay the other side of the valley, covered in tall trees, a rather elegant redbrick building set amid the forest which he had seen that morning during the carriageride to the river. The view was serene in the fleeting brilliance of the late summer afternoon beams; there was an urgency, a kind of pleading in the very beauty of it, the blue sky darkening, the colours mellowing, everything hushed and stilled by the unspoken theme, the feeling that it all was ending. Melancholy ripening like a swollen fruit, its heavy dark radiation penetrating through walls, through skulls, stalked its progenitor sunbeams, those rays falling risingly on the forsaken leaves, rising fallingly up the trees towards infinity: the last achyloving throws of a soon setting sun.

- 14 -
The Portrait

Calpurnia started playing another tune: this song was sadly pretty, reverently contemplative, a delicate motif descending leaflike twice and then swept upwards as by an impassioned wave, dropped further, and swept up once more and thrown higher into the air where it dallied, dominant, a while in sprightly dissonant exhilaration before recommencing from the start.

Tom took a last look at the sunlit valley, sighed, stood back, and, without meaning to, fixed his eyes upon a portrait, a little smaller than the window, hanging on the wall to the right. Tom moved closer to get a good look at the portrait: it was a painted picture of a young woman, beautiful with light brown hair combed back behind her ears, clear pale skin blushing faintly in the cheeks, and large, somewhat feline bluegrey eyes. Tom, vulnerably saturnine, became immediately enchanted with the picture as soon as his eyes fell upon it. The mouth was not quite smiling, but the woman's face cast an aura of great happiness (in fact, Tom could not remember seeing such pure untroubled joy in a face since he had spoken with Peter Gardener that morning) which was the essence of the beauty: the happiness seemed to permeate her flesh, her hair, her orange dress, unworried, unquestioned, sure. The black hole pupils of her eyes seemed to peer through the canvas from another long-forgotten but familiar dimension; they had a powerful magnetic force which pulled Tom forward like a puppet on a string, his hands resting on the wall on either side of the portrait, the better to lean in, the better to keep himself from falling in. Tom could not understand the woman's beauty: it was not traceable to any detectable trick or special skill of the painter, and it seemed to be well beyond the scope of artistic rendering; it seemed to inhabit the painting, almost *behind* the painting, in the otherworldly eternity of mesmerizing darkness in her eyes. The wooden-framed canvas seemed like it could not bear the weight of the beauty it bore, and seemed about to fall tearing into shreds to the floor. Tom knew without a doubt (for what was doubt now?) that he knew the face, the eyes, the dark eternity behind the paltry world of matter which concealed it, shamed red and shaky by the sheer hopelessness of concealing.

And he knew that he was in love with the woman – was, in that ancient empty void which existed before this current congested void; was, now, a love ever lurking beneath the endlessly layered fiasco of his dreamworld; would forever be in love with the woman. The recognition filled him with a rush of delight, and his inflating head filled with warm tender thoughts of her: simpler thoughts of going places, to castles, fields, forests, lakes, rivers, oceans, islands, dark city streets, bright tower-tops, and more, knowing he had done it all before and would do it all again; thoughts of swimming in her otherworldly gaze, generous eyelashes sharing sharply, the whites of her eyes professing their lady's sublimity, the galaxies of her pupils filled with everlasting promises; thoughts of looking at her: the slopes rolling down from her cheekbones were supple fields of paradise, falling unwittingly over the ridge of a narrowing covetable chin, or, luckier, coming to rest in the softer cushiony ravine of her closed lips. A love whose heaving breath heaves long enough to while away eternity, trapped in loving thought, imprisoned.

An oubliette. Tom's heart sank: he knew that she was dead; she was nowhere to be found in flesh. The presence which had gazed on him hard upon his first entering the house originated in this terrible portrait, this portrait alone, and Tom's heart broke into a whirlpool of pain. He felt it in his chest like a gunshot, blowing away all that warmth, all that gladness (all that love which in its very boundlessness of being ensured the fatality of this ultimate toll); he felt it in his gut like an explosion, blowing away all that peace, leaving inhuman unendurable chaos.

Tom sank slowly, his heart wrenched, his gut in turmoil, his hands dragging down the wall, until he fell onto his knees, but he did not stop there; he sank further, his spine collapsing, his shoulders slumping dead, his arms loosely falling, his fingers weakly clawing, tumbling silently sideways and rolling up, his muscles moving in jerks, covering his head with his arms and pulling his legs into his stomach, to the first and final position. He could not cry, though he wanted.to; he wanted to scream the world away, but knew that he could not; he wanted to die, but could not think how. In love with a ghost? How could it happen? Why did it happen, to me, just now? In love with a ghost? His mouth spoke the words, but he was gone far beyond thinking, to a world reserved only for the cursed, a pain beyond reckoning, a hell beyond escape.

Tom shook in his heap, himself, for a long time, the remainder of the song, which was a long time because Calpurnia went through the chord progression many times, performing many improvisations thereover, very impressive, certainly prodigious, while Tom shuddered on the carpet. Infernal images swept over his blurred vision; all of the blood left his limbs, his torso, and rushed into his forehead where it boiled and stirred violently in tempestuous rebellion; a raspy moan sounded from his bloodless blueing lips.

When the song ended, Tom automatically tried to reassess the situation, not believing that it was true. He strained his eyes upwards towards the portrait quickly, putting considerable stress on his levator palpebrae superiori and very nearly breaking his lateral recti, surprising the hell out of his superior, medial, and inferior recti, but the portrait was still there, and the terrible presence still oozed out of it at full force, if possible stronger than before. Her eyes seemed to be straining down on him, tyrannical, evilly insistent; Tom gave himself up to another little fit of lovepainspasms, and then threw himself onto his feet and rushed down the stairs, his feet heavy like concrete and his muscles fevered, and into the room where they had entered. Seeing Calpurnia sitting on the piano bench, her legs dangling swingingly, contemplating which song to play next, he cried, "Calpurnia, you evil girl, why did you bring me into this terrible house?" His breath was heavy and fraught by the feeling of hurt, of heartbreak.

Calpurnia slowly slid herself leftwards down the piano bench, turned herself sideways so she was facing off the west side of the bench, and then jumped off and turned with a little skip and looked at Tom and said, "Don't worry about Nilly; she tries that one on every one."

Calpurnia clearly did not understand. Tom cried, "But I love her!"

"Well, that's an awful waste of time ... and energy! She's been dead over a hundred years!"

Tom covered his face with his hands and started to make loud gruff noises of grievous mental disruption interspersed with desperate wheezing exhalations. Once he started in this way he took to it wholeheartedly and continued thus until he heard the light tapping of notes on the piano. At first the notes deepened his distress, and then Calpurnia played a particular melody, a short one-bar musical statement and Tom unexpectedly, miraculously, unbelievably, felt his body clear of the unendurable pain of love.

- 15 -
The Equinox Feast

At first Tom did not believe it was happening, and then there was no need for him to believe, for it had already happened. He felt fine again: there was no love, no heart-bleeding, no gut-wrenching, anymore. For a brief moment after it had passed he felt somehow artificial, as though he had been made aware just for an instant of some great cosmic deception, as though a mask whose reality he had always taken for granted had been removed just for a second, the mousy wearer had peeked out and winked at him from beneath, and then had quickly replaced the mask and carried on with the charade as if nothing had happened. But the wound was healed, the pain was gone, leaving not even a scar.

Dropping his hands from his face, Tom said, "Calpurnia, how did you do that?"

Calpurnia slid down the piano bench and hopped off and turned to him again, this time with a knowing mischievous smile, and said, "I am afraid, Tom, that that is a secret. It is a very special technique which I learned about during my clandestine investigations through the libraries in the house."

Tom thought it best not to inquire further, and said thankfully, "Calpurnia, I don't know what I would do without you. *You* are the true Solstice Hero!"

Calpurnia seemed to remember something as Tom said these words, and she looked at the window, the beams of light flowing therethrough becoming increasingly horizontal and yellow, and said, "We need to get back to the house before the feast begins! Since you are the Solstice Hero, it's your job to seed Mother."

Tom was surprised to hear this, but he was not at all against the idea of more sex, feeling well-energized; but remembering Mother's decapitation, he said, "But Mother is dead."

"Yes," Calpurnia said in her familiar tone of boredom, "I'm not sure how Ronny's going to figure that out. At worst they will have to choose another Mother, but that would be risky since it would have to be a woman whose health hasn't been so closely monitored, blah blah blah, Tom I don't give a fuck it's your problem."

Calpurnia went over to the window and pulled it open and placed the short plank under it and climbed outside. Tom followed her, his feet first this time, which was a little easier, and then once he got outside he asked her, "Calpurnia, what was that tune you were playing, that second one, the one when I was upstairs?"

"It's a favourite of mine: it's called *In Your Own Sweet Way* by Dave Brubeck," she replied, replacing the plank under the sill and letting the window down softly; then she said, sighing wistfully, "It always makes me think of Nitskee."

"Ah. I think it made me fall in love with Nilly; at least it contributed to my downfall."

"Sorry about that."

"It's okay."

Tom picked up the bucket of raspberries and they started heading back to camp. Tom noticed that it was significantly cooler now: late summer had given way to autumn, and Tom thought that he must have spent a very long time in that house (and in fact he had been in there nearly two hours). The sun was orange now, sinking low into the horizon, and Tom knew that it would set very soon. The leaves were turning: some unhealthier trees had already burned through their last and now stood naked in the crisp cooling air; most were halfway gone, red, yellow, orange and brown, beautiful by day to the careless young, but revealed in the dark to be deathly at heart. Birds were beginning their migrations.

The front yard of the house was empty, and Tom heard a medley of voices coming from the backyard. The party seemed to have already begun, and Tom wondered what Ronny's brilliant idea was. They headed to the backyard, and saw that the bonfire had been relit and a crowd was amassing around it, talking youngly and excitedly. One of the youths saw them coming and cried, "Tom has returned! Our Equinox Seeder has arrived!" and the whole crowd turned and started cheering and clapping, some more forward ones coming up and offering Tom their felicitous hands for shaking. Tom ignored them, and looked around for Ronny, but the boy was nowhere to be seen in the yard of darkening faces (for the trees of the neighbourhood were many and tall, and by now the sun was only visible from the open street).

Tom noticed that Calpurnia had disappeared, which she seemed always to do when he found himself mobbed, but luckily he saw George (Tom might easily have avoided the whole thing by leaving, but he wanted to become acquainted with his new duties); George came up to him and said, "Come this way, please, sir," and led Tom towards the bonfire. Tom cast a glance at the shed, which was no longer an object of the youths' attention, as they passed it, and he thought he could see a white blur in the dirty window, but was not sure; the padlock was still on the door. When they got to the bonfire Tom saw that bear meat was cooking on a spit, and a young man was seated in an old plastic lawn-chair playing guitar not very well; the many youths were flitting around the flickering flames of the bonfire, some in talkative groups, many drinking from glasses or eating food from plates.

George led Tom to a group of three young women on the north side of the bonfire who were standing at a remove from the rest of the party. All were dressed in long plain white dresses, and all three were healthy-looking and pretty, but none stood out as more so than the others, except that Tom recognized one as the young woman who had approached him earlier and offered to take him for a relaxing walk; she smiled at him, and Tom smiled back, although he was a little bashful now.

George said to Tom, "Here you go: make your choice, and then go do your thing over there," – he gestured towards the man-sized hole in the northeast corner of the hedge – "in the house next-door. You will find all you need in the kitchen."

Tom chose the one he recognized; she came forward and held his hand and said, "We meet again."

Then George asked, "Are you hungry?"

Tom thought about this for a moment. He did not feel as superpowerful as he had felt last time in the woods, and thought maybe some bear meat would do the trick; he was about to ask for a bear meat sandwich when a little black ball of energy bounced into their midst and burst out into the form of Ronny, and yelled, "Wait a minute! There have been some last-minute changes!"

Everyone jumped back in surprise, and then, realizing who it was, waited for Ronny to explain; once he knew that they had all adapted to his presence, Ronny said, "I have, with much hard work and considerable mental strain, managed to accomplish a rare miracle! A great achievement which will be remembered for as long as our people continue to flourish in this valley: a reclamation from the cold clutches of death ... the reviving of Mother!"

As he said this, he turned and gestured with both hands pointing proudly back towards the house, and they all turned and saw, to their great astonishment, Jack leading a woman dressed in Mother's blue dress, with Mother's voluptuous figure underneath, who seemed in every way to be Mother except that she had a paper bag on her head and she walked unsteadily, drunkenly, and looked like she would fall down without the help of Jack. As she approached, Tom saw, drawn on the front of the bag by what appeared to be crayon, a ridiculous face consisting of a big orange circle, with brown streaks scribbled around the top for hair, in which floated two big lopsided blue eyes, an orange V for a nose, and an absurd crooked red semicircle for a smile, and he laughed.

Ronny smirked embarrassedly, looked at the ground sheepishly, and said, "Drawing has never been my forte."

Tom suppressed his laughter and looked at Ronny with spread eyebrows in expectation of further explanation.

"You see, her head needs to remain covered as a medical precaution, and she is not quite fully ... with us yet," Ronny said, patting Mother's shoulder. Then, swelling with joyful pride, he said loudly, "But she should make a full recovery! The body has not been compromised, so she will be able to fulfill her purpose. The show must go on!"

First Jack, who seemed very impressed with Ronny, said, "Good job, Ronny!" and then George started clapping and murmuring approbation, and he was joined by the three girls and Tom, and then the whole crowd was cheering and shouting hurrahs for Ronny.

Then, once they had all settled down again, Ronny looked up at Tom and said, "Well, do your thing."

Tom looked uncertainly at Mother, whom Jack was pushing in his direction, and in a moment she was in his arms, and he had to struggle to hold her up. He thought he heard her say, in a muffled voice that sounded much rougher than the high-pitched one that had welcomed him that morning, "A judgement of taste, just as if it were merely subjective, cannot be determined by bases of proof ..."

Tom thought this was weird, but he remembered that Ronny had said she was still not in her right head. At least she was alive. Later she could show him around the house, perhaps. Tom felt more than a little reluctant to have sex with her in such a state, but as everyone was prodding him on and cheering him, he thought he might as well enjoy himself with her: he was, after all, the Equinox Seeder, and if it was not him it would be someone else; this was her purpose, for which she had been preparing all summer, was it not?; and he thought that if he should at the last minute lose heart, or potency, or be troubled by an unexpected qualm of conscience, he could simply run away and leave the seeding to someone else. He led her towards the hedge, and shot a last look back at the group; they were all smiling at him encouragingly, but he detected a strange look on Ronny's face when he looked at Mother, a worry which seemed almost to be one born of devious deception; but Tom dismissed it as nothing, as a technical worry concerning the state of Mother's health, and he smiled at the group as he led Mother through the hole in the hedge and into the next yard.

The next yard was large and dozens of trees grew thickly therein; it was practically a forest. Tom could barely see southwards through the trees that the backdoor to the house was open, and the inside of the house looked tidy, as though someone had cleaned it up for him, and he remembered George saying that everything he needed would be in there; he led Mother towards the backdoor, the dry dead leaves crackling under their feet.

He thought it polite to give Mother a chance to back out, and he said, "Mother, it is my great privilege as Equinox Seeder to ... seed you now."

Mother, wobbling unsteadily and swaying heavily into and away from him like a drunk, said, in the same rough, raspy voice, "Let's do it."

Tom laughed, "Are you sure?"

"Absolutely."

Tom thought he should maybe test her to see if she was really fully conscious; he said, "How old is Father?"

"Far too old! That's for sure!" she laughed raspingly, spurring a wet hacking cough.

"How many years?"

"One hundred and thirteen, and nine months and ... almost twenty-eight days!"

Tom now felt adequately satisfied that Mother was in possession of her senses. As a final courtesy, he asked, "Are you sure you can handle a ... seeding right now? Would you not rather postpone it?"

Mother said, in a surprisingly deep, coarse, demanding voice, "No! It is crucial that it be done now! Come on, worm, get it done!" Tom looked at her curiously, a little frightened and quite put off; then Mother said, in a softer but still raspy voice, "Well ... I mean, if you want to ... I mean, if you would be so kind, my dear."

Tom looked closely at the bag over her head and the absurd cartoon drawn upon it. He wanted to see her face; it was irking him greatly; he would feel so much better about the whole thing if he could see her face. The only thing that stopped him from pulling the bag off her head was consideration for her health, as Ronny had warned him against doing so; so he said, "Maybe a pastille would help with your throat."

"Probably; thanks for your kindness," she said.

Tom helped her up the few steps into the back of the house and they entered a kitchen with a single candle, lit, on the cleared counter, with bare white walls, and with a small cot where the table should have been against the south wall at the foot of which sat a black leather doctor's bag.

Here we go, thought Tom to himself, but he was now extremely reluctant to carry out his duty, not at all aroused by Mother's bizarre state; he wanted the old Mother back; maybe tomorrow she would be in better health, and he could take that accursed bag off her head? Mother was now staggering uncontrollably and Tom led her over to the bed and sat her down so that he could think what to do next. To hell with it, he thought, I should just run away; to heck with these kids; to heck with this place.

Tom was not amused when Mother rolled over clumsily onto her stomach and began reaching down at the bottom of her blue dress in a pathetically uncoordinated attempt to pull it up; she said, still in her rough deep voice, "Please don't mind if I talk philosophy while we do it; Kant turns me on." Tom edged back towards the door, thinking there was definitely something wrong with her, thinking of running for it; she continued, "If someone does not find a building, a view, or a poem beautiful, then, first, he will refuse to let even a hundred voices, all praising it highly, prod him into approving of it inwardly. He may of course act as if he liked it too," – she coughed harshly – "so that people will not think that he lacks taste. He may even begin to doubt whether he has in fact done enough to mold his taste," – she managed at last to grab a corner of her dress with her left hand and pull it up revealing her plumpish, white, sexy left thigh and most of her right leg, and Tom looked away, embarrassed – "by familiarizing himself with a sufficient number of objects of a certain kind (just as someone who thinks he recognizes a forest in some distant object that everyone else regards as a town will doubt the judgement of his own eyes). And yet he realizes clearly that other people's approval in no way provides him with a valid proof by which to judge beauty;" – she managed to grab a corner on the other side of her dress with her right hand, and began pulling it up until her legs were fully exposed, and Tom (no longer looking away) came forward with the intention of stopping her from revealing her bum – "even though others may perhaps see and observe for him, and even though what many have seen the same way may serve him, who believes he saw it differently –"[2]

---

[2] Mother is quoting a passage from Section 33 of Immanuel Kant's *Critique of Judgment*.

Here Tom grabbed her by her left shoulder and rolled her over, saying, "Stop it!" and when he did he got a tremendous shock: the paper bag on her head ripped and came off, and Tom saw something he had not at all expected, and he thought at first that some terrible thing had happened to her head because the bag had come off, and began apologizing remorsefully, until he realized that he was looking at Father's damp scarred wrinkled gleaming bald brown head sewn grotesquely to Mother's soft white unblemished neck, a swan with a vulture's head – both Tom's and Father's heads screamed at once.

They went on screaming for a long time, staring at each other wide-eyed, all four hands waving around wildly, until Tom stopped screaming and lowered his hands in downwardwaving calming movements, and Father began to quieten too; they both realized that they had not been formally introduced.

"After you, sir," said Tom.

FatherMother tried to sit up, but had great difficulty, so Tom politely helped it up; once FatherMother was sitting up, Father said, "My name is Albert," and tried to extend Mother's right hand towards Tom, but instead her hand went a foot to the right of Tom's stomach, pointing northwestwards.

Tom reached out and took Mother's hand and said, "Nice to meet you, sir; my name is Tom."

At these words Mother's right hand let go of Tom's and began making its way towards Albert's chin, the forefinger began to scratch before it had reached its destination, and then it never reached its destination and began scratching at the air under and before his chin, and Albert's goblinish features grimaced and squinted and scowled in what appeared to be deep, and not untroubled, thought. Tom waited patiently, inwardly snickering, while Albert performed these ghoulishly comedic movements, Mother's right forefinger trying tirelessly to scratch his chin but never ever making it.

Finally Albert arched his ancient eyebrows and looked at Tom and said, after a cough and a gulp, "Tom? Where are you from?"

Tom answered, "Well, you see, I am the Equinox Seeder. But Peter Gardener sent me, before that."

At these words Albert's jaw dropped in surprise, exposing a set of white dentures, and he exclaimed, "But that is impossible! I gave clear instructions that you were to be brought to me as soon as you arrived! And now you are the Equinox Seeder? How could this happen?" He looked around and yelled, "Mother! You useless cow!" and then, seeming to remember (or realize for the first time) the circumstances of his embodiment, he looked down at Mother's body, her hands having dropped to its sides, and frowned at it.

Tom said, "Well, here I am."

"Is it too late?"

"Is it too late for what?"

Albert squinted in second thought and tried again, "Let me see ... er, how did you come to occupy the position of Equinox Seeder?" he made a grimace of tremendous effort and Mother's right hand came up and landed with a wet slap on his right cheek, making him flinch in pain before he looked at Tom questioningly in what appeared to be an effort to look unthreatening and friendly.

Tom thought back through his day, which had been an odd one, and answered, "Well, I met Ronny and the others at the stream, and then I met Mother, and then I went for a hunt with Ronny and Calpurnia, and then ... oh yes: then I killed the bear, and then was declared Solstice Hero for my pains, and then we came back and had lunch, and then ... oh yes: there was that awful tragedy when Summa beheaded Mother –"

"Wait a minute!" Albert interrupted, "Did you say Summa beheaded Mother?"

Tom nodded, "Yes, that's right."

"Good God! Just as the *Portentus Stomachi* predicted!"

"Predicted?" Tom remembered at this moment what Summa had said in the woods about the story she had read on HP's face, and he looked at Albert sharply, worried about how much he knew; to his dismay, Albert's eyes were bulging at him in wild fury.

"Predicted!" Father's head exclaimed, and Mother's body began jerking itself towards the foot of the cot where the black leather doctor's bag sat, her arms hitting the mattress for propulsion and her feet pushing on the floor, and Albert's face contorted into a look of extreme effort and determination, his false teeth bared and his eyes narrowed to furious little slits. "How could I have been so blind?"

Tom was confused and rather frightened; he wondered what Albert was trying to do with the doctor's bag. "What are you doing?" he asked.

"Oh nothing, my boy, just getting some meds," Albert growled, but Tom did not believe him and started backing towards the door. When most of his body was out the door, he left his head in the room just to see what Albert would take out of the bag, but it took a long time for Albert even just to manoeuvre Mother's right hand up to the doctor's bag, landing near the left buckle, and Tom knew that the chances of Father's accessing the inside of the bag with Mother's hands, let alone finding anything therein, in under twenty-four hours were slim at best.

"Can I help you with that, sir?" Tom asked, sarcastically as he knew that Father did not approve of him, not at all.

Father let Mother's right hand fall down onto the bed and looked at Tom's head in the doorway and said defeatedly, "Get Ronny over here, will you?"

Tom said, "Okay, sir. I'll be back in a jiffy."

He removed his head from the room and turned and walked towards the hole in the hedge at the back of the yard. He heard Albert muttering in the room behind him, "I should have known something was amiss when Ronny ... but never this ... Experiment he says! Natural causes! I'll give him an experiment."

Tom picked up his pace, and as he walked he considered what to do next. He understood now what Ronny's worried look had been about: Ronny had pulled a fast one on him, and Tom did not appreciate it, not at all. He considered giving Ronny a berating, but realized that everyone would want to know what he had done with Mother, and why he was back so soon; thus he expected Ronny to guess immediately what had happened, and thought he shouldn't even go back to the camp at all. Run away he most certainly would have done, but three things held him back: firstly, he wanted to see what was happening with Summa; secondly, he wanted to find Calpurnia and tell her that he was leaving, and thank her for her help; thirdly, he wanted to get some food, for he was beginning to feel the strain of the excitement and shock of the most recent events on his body, and wanted a full stomach, and possibly full pockets also, for his impending flight.

Thus Tom poked his head through the hole in the hedge to make sure that no-one was looking in his direction, hoping for as much time as possible before being approached by Ronny or some other suspicious young person. He saw, to his surprise, that no-one was around the fire. He poked his head out further and saw that all of the youths, strangely silent, were gathered around the shed next to the hedge to the south in which Summa had been locked. No-one said a word, and they all stood still, some swaying a little. Tom wondered what was happening with Summa, and hoped everything was all right. However, he first exploited their absence from around the fire by stealing over quietly to a plate of bear meat sandwiches, stuffing one into each of his jeans' forepockets, and then taking a third in his right hand and grabbing with his left hand a handful of lettuce from a nearby bowl, and taking a big bite out of the sandwich. He stood for a moment by the bonfire, eating the sandwich and looking at the youths, none of whom had yet turned and noticed him, and tried to discern from their actions what was happening in the shed. They were all staring silently, seriously, seemingly transfixed by whatever was happening.

The sun had set while he had been in the house next door: he had missed its last rays. The air was cold; the wind was picking up; the leaves were falling all around him, spinning in little whirlwinds; and an eery windy silence had settled over the populous yard. Tom thought it rather risky to go over there, a very bad idea, but he needed to know what was happening. His curiosity finally got the better of him, and he decided to go over there, but first he got a mug of water and gulped it down, and finished off the sandwich and the lettuce; that would have to do for now. He began walking over to the group of youths gathered around the shed.

No-one noticed him as he approached from behind, so transfixed were they by whatever they were seeing, and Tom walked right up to the group. The youths were nodding slowly, their mouths hanging open, and some of them were whispering inaudibly to themselves like opiated dreamers. Tom could tell instinctively that they were every one possessed by that bewilderment of seeing the never-before-seen, the never-believed-possible, and Tom knew that in such a state they were not likely to think rationally about his early return and what it implied regarding Mother, Albert, FatherMother; thus he felt confident enough to ask one what was going on, as he could not see for himself over their shoulders and heads, but was dying to find out ...

"What's going on?" he asked a youth, who appeared to be in his early teens. The youth turned his head slowly revealing his clear hairless face, and slowly fixed his eyes, aghast, on Tom, seemed about to say something, but then seemed to decide against it, shook his head, and turned his head forward again and began staring at the back of the person ahead of him; clearly the boy knew what was going on, but lacked either the energy, the courage, or the descriptive abilities needed to relate it. Tom started pushing his way through the youths, all of whom were similarly dumbfounded, until he broke through the crowd; when he pushed by the shoulders of the last youths, he saw the object of their beholding, and got a tremendous shock.

It was Summa: she was lying on the ground, propped up by her elbows, her legs opened into a V over the ground, crushed under the massive weight of her enormous stomach, a mass ten times her own size, five feet tall by five feet wide, the mysterious bulge grown to extreme proportions. Her jeans had been let open and pulled down a little and her white T-shirt was pushed up and bundled on her chest to allow for the bulge. She looked up as Tom broke through the crowd, and stared at him emptily. No-one said anything.

The mass was growing before their eyes: it seemed to grow by five to ten percent in the few seconds Tom was looking at it. Tom immediately started backing away from Summa as soon as she fixed him with her gaze; her eyes were empty, lobotomized, far beyond appall. Tom fell headfirst through the crowd, swimming backwards away from Summa through the stunned unresponsive bodies. When he emerged he spun around, downwardtending, and fell onto his hands and knees like a sun-stroked figure-skater. "That can't be good," he said to the grass.

A moment later he sensed the ever-energetic presence of Ronny at his side, and heard Ronny's voice in its most frantic mode, "Tom, you've never heard of anything like this – I mean ... oh, never mind; how did it go with Mother?"

"Mother was a great sport," answered Tom automatically, still on all fours, then added, "She is tired right now, and requested that she be left alone for a half-hour to better ... process the new ... information – I mean, process the new seed ... of information ..." Tom trailed off, unconsciously crawling away from the silently staring crowd.

"Did anything ... untoward happen?" Ronny asked, a note of uneasiness.

"Ha! Are you kidding? It was a most straightforwardly splendid seeding – this is going to be a good one!" Tom finally pushed himself onto his feet with a clumsy shove and stumbled away from Ronny, never even looking at his face.

Tom careened away, unbalanced, across the backyard and around the corner of the house and landed with his back leaned against its western side. The wind threw his hair around and covered him with splashes of coolness. He closed his eyes for a moment and inhaled deeply, and in the backdrop of his mind saw Summa, lying back on her elbows, staring blankly at him from underneath the growing mass. What is going on? What is it?

Tom, deciding to run for it once and for all, opened his eyes to see Calpurnia's scornful face eyeing him scrutinizingly. "What's the matter this time, you big baby?" she sneered, then smiled, gaptoothed.

Tom shook his head and said, "We have to get out of here, Calpurnia. Something terrible has happened ... is about to happen ... is happening!"

To Tom's surprise, Calpurnia nodded earnestly and said, "I'm coming with you, Tom; you won't make it five minutes out there."

"Great! Let's go!"

"Okay!" Calpurnia said simply; then, to Tom's greater surprise, she picked up a duffel bag and threw it at him and said, "Supplies!"

Tom caught the bag, slung it over his shoulder, and began fleeing down the driveway. When he reached the end of the driveway he heard Calpurnia's voice, elevated, say, "Ahem, aren't you forgetting something?"

Tom looked back and saw that Calpurnia had mounted the driver's seat of the carriage; a moment later the carriage backed up quickly and nearly ran over Tom's left toes, before Tom could even react to it.

"Come on! You don't want to be hunted like an animal, do you?"

Tom pulled himself up to the driver's seat beside Calpurnia, and when he sat down next to her he heard a yell from the backyard of the house. The yell was followed by more yells and shouts, and then he heard screaming, followed next by all the noises of commotion and uproar: it sounded like every voice, no matter what age or gender, was equally terrified, and they were all moving, fleeing. Then Tom heard screams of a higher kind: screams of extreme terror and excruciating pain, sustained wails piercing through the wind, ending abruptly, and then replaced by different screams of greater terror and greater pain.

The carriage lurched into motion, and they began clopping hastily up the road just as Tom saw some youths running, their faces broken by terror, around the side of the house towards them, yelling, "Help us!" "Wait for me!" and "Don't leave me!"

"Kiss my ass, you curs!" called Calpurnia as the horses broke into a canter and pulled them away beyond reach. Tom, looking back towards the portion of backyard visible behind the house, thought he saw the top half of a body, severed at the waist, arms flailing and followed by a tail of intestines, flying through the air out from the backyard into the next yard westwards; but he was not sure, as it was becoming darker. He turned back and looked up the windy darkening road, hearing Calpurnia chuckle triumphantly, "They'll never catch us."

- 16 -
Suche die Höhen

Tom was very glad to escape. He felt that he had left at the right time, and had taken the best thing, the only thing worth keeping, with him: his friend Calpurnia. He did not want to think about what was happening behind him in the camp; he knew only that whatever it was, it was bad. It was satisfying to leave that world behind without even a second look back; Tom felt a great exhilaration of escape, accentuated by the windy darkness of the autumn evening, his hair whipping in the wind, his shirt flapping on his lucky body. His breast swelled with the excitement of the moment, and between gasps he exclaimed, "Calpurnia! You're my hero!"

Calpurnia rolled her eyes, but stared straightfaced ahead of them, her cruelly bent eyebrows lowered in masterful conviction. Rather than turning left at the redbrick house as they had done that morning, they went up the road and then took the first road turning right, called Bown. After going northwards two blocks they turned left onto a road called Maple, and then took the first right onto a road called Price, which took them to the outskirts of the town (for behind the houses to the left of the road stood tall dark forest, dark ghostly forest, no more suburbia) and which curved rightwards, northeastwards towards the river. Then eventually the road joined with a main road, or highway, which headed northwest out of town; there was a final little gas station across the street. Calpurnia did not stop, but kept the horses cantering, encouraging them at times with gentle whips at the reins. The horses pounded along proudly, their full bodies plodding effortlessly, pulling the carriage smoothly, floatingly like a cloud through the thin air.

Tom was getting cold. He rubbed his arms with their opposite hands as the road began going uphill and the wind intensified. It was getting dark quickly; the departing light left in its place an unforgiving sharp chill. The streetlights stood like sinister tall spectres, their unignitable orbs drooping mournfully over the road. The moon, large and almost full save a small slice shorn off its left side, hung low and orange in the eastern sky, its bottom glow troubled by the languorous march of the trees, leafless or coniferous, on the hill across the valley. The darkness was descending, settling into the earth; the Equinox passed; wintry nighttime manifesting, a heavy slowly seeping flood of black, a blinding mass of flavourless intangible molasses. The whole visible world was becoming less and less visible, less and less knowable with every chilling breath. The infant melancholia of high summer had long budded and metamorphosed into a pale blue petrification: its butterfly wings were delicate thin shards of ice, its growing pains eclipsed by the recent confusion of the Equinox Feast; but, beneath the rush of wind, the heartpounding excitement, the knowledge that terrible things were happening behind, Tom knew now well what frozen fossil stared walleyed from under the window of black ice (or mirror?) at the foot of his heart and he felt every other warm emotion gliding slowly off over the slippery ledge into winter's harrowing way.

And then it was done: night was complete, leaving only the clear spellbinding light of the stars and the low orange orb of the moon behind them in the eastern sky. The road was going gradually uphill, curving into the west along with the river, and they passed by dim grey buildings now and again, lurking at the side of the road like the lost or the mad, harkening with a start at the approach of the carriage and freezing still as it passed.

Tom was getting very cold; he said to Calpurnia, "Calpurnia, I'm freezing! Do we have a sweater or something I can put on?"

Calpurnia rolled her eyes and looked over at Tom impatiently; then she said, "I suppose." She whoahed the horses to a stop and said, "In the back compartment you will find all you need." Then after a pause she added, "Bring me a jacket too!"

Tom climbed down from the driver's seat and looked around at the night. They were now well into the countryside, and there was no building in sight at this place. Tom went to the rear of the carriage and opened a little latch on the door to the back compartment and threw it open, revealing a fairly large cavity which went under the back seat of the carriage; at the right many knives, spears, swords and hatchets were piled neatly, and at the left was packed compactly an assortment of folded shirts, jackets, pants and blankets, and a few hats and toques strayed about. Tom chose a long blue jacket, a thick brown jacket for Calpurnia, a brown woolen sweater, and he took a heavy grey toque for good measure; he did not know how cold it would get atop the carriage, and he was already beginning to shiver. After shutting the back compartment he went with his bundle back to his place in the driver's seat, sending a quick look over his shoulder before he sat down: the town was well out of sight; only the black looming shoulders of the forest hovered on the horizon at either side of the vanishing point of the road. To the north were sprinkled the million stars whitely on the river, downhill, on the other side of a few hundred meters of downwardsloping dark.

The carriage lurched into motion. Tom placed the thick brown jacket beside Calpurnia; Calpurnia said nothing. That abundant life hidden in the surrounding darkness seemed to be receding slowly into hibernation, sinking further into sleep with every dropping degree. Tom put the sweater on, and, deciding that he was still cold, threw the blue jacket over it and stuffed the toque into the left inside pocket, for he enjoyed the feeling of the cool wind in his hair. This reminded him of the bear meat sandwiches stuffed damply in his jeans' forepockets, and he laughed at the thought, and decided that he had done very well indeed. Never mind whatever unimaginable pain, what ineffable insanity was taking place behind him around the house; it was not his problem. The kids were nice enough; the food was good; the sex had been a pleasant surprise. Never mind the rest, never mind it. Tom pulled the sandwich from his right pocket and took a bite out of it; then, thinking of the driver, he said, "Calpurnia, do you want a bear meat sandwich? It has been tarnished somewhat by the inside of my pocket; sorry –"

But at that moment Calpurnia yelled "Whoah!" and the horses stopped their cantering and the carriage halted.

"What is it, Calpurnia?" Tom asked her, a little frightened at the abruptness of her command. They had stopped about fifteen feet before a modern steel and concrete bridge. The dark asphalt shone with a faint red gleam in studded reflection of the light of the moon, which was rising slowly in the sky, and the ardent stars.

Calpurnia said nothing, and Tom could see that she was staring ahead at something on the right side of the road; she looked frightened, Tom realized, and this frightened him even more because he had never seen Calpurnia frightened and he didn't like seeing it. He looked with a jolt at the side of the road and at first could not see anything; then, sending a sudden bolt of panic up his spine, he saw a figure, dressed all in black but with his suit left open revealing a white shirt beneath, his shoulders darker among the dark pine-trees, take three steps out onto the road. The figure held a walking stick but was not using it for support, but was rather tapping it softly and dragging it at times lightly back and forth over the pavement in a ponderous way. Tom could barely see his face in the unsubstantial light, but he could make out an extremely large moustache, the tawny weeds of at least one year's growth, but probably much more, concealing the entire lower half of his face. Tom knew that the man was looking at the carriage, but he could not see the man's eyes. Tom blurted shakily, "What do you want? Come no nearer! I have a gun in my pocket."

The man said nothing, but did not step, but kept staring in their direction. He brought his head down and forward to get a better look at the carriage. After a few moments Calpurnia said, "What is your name?"

The man finally spoke, "Englisch? Uh ... er, Why was I so frightened in my dream that I ... awoke? Did not a child carrying a ... Spiegel come to me?" His voice was scratchy and wet and worn, sickly, and he had a heavy Prussian accent (but of course Tom simply thought of it as foreign).

Tom thought his words made no sense, and he began worrying that perhaps the man was dangerous or insane, and he looked uneasily at Calpurnia, hoping that she would know what to do. To Tom's surprise, he saw that Calpurnia's face was lit up with excitement, giving off its own pale glow; she said, in a rapturous voice, "O Zarathustra, look at yourself in the mirror!" and she leapt off the carriage and ran over to the man, crying, "Nitskeeee!" and jumped up and threw her arms around his shoulders.

Friedrich Nietzsche staggered and fell back, and the two became a confused blob for a few moments before Tom could again distinguish the shorter brighter shape of Calpurnia from the taller darker shape of Nietzsche. Apparently he was not dead, but alive and out for an evening stroll. The two began talking, but Tom could not make out their words, only the tone. Calpurnia was talking quickly, fervently, and Nietzsche was making deeper abashed sounds, happy; this went on for a while, and then Calpurnia slowed down and started speaking more composedly and seriously for a while; then there was silence, a note of tension; then Nietzsche started speaking, slowly but steadily, a fairly long speech; and then there was more silence. Calpurnia said something quietly, then Nietzsche said something quietly; then Calpurnia said something else, and Nietzsche said something else; then Nietzsche bent over and Calpurnia stepped forward and they hugged, and then Nietzsche turned and disappeared into the darkness of the pines and Calpurnia stood for a few moments and watched him depart. She stood there for a few moments after he had departed, then she looked up at the sky; she craned her neck back and stood on her toes, lost her balance a little and regained it, and then she stood for as long as she could on her toes, waveringly, the pale light of the stars and the moon drawing wraithlike her small shaky form, before she came back down onto her heels and turned slowly back towards Tom and began walking, slowly, back to the carriage.

She climbed slowly up the side of the carriage, and as she sat she said, "My heart is dead." Tom saw the gleam of tears in her eyes, and he was so taken aback that he didn't know what to say (not that he thought anything was needed, or wanted). Calpurnia sat quietly and looked off the side of the road at the darkness into which Nietzsche had disappeared, a look of pain, for several long moments. Tom looked off at the nighttime view: over the bridge the road stretched onwards, upwards into the west, bordered at either side by the tall trees. He wished Calpurnia would stop crying; he felt strangely undermined by this sudden breakdown of his hitherto seemingly imperturbable heroine, like a firm foundation had collapsed completely and left him hanging in mid-air. Calpurnia continued to say nothing, but stared quietly, blinking away the tears at times, her slight shoulders shuddering every few moments.

Finally Tom reached his left hand out and put it on her right shoulder and said, "What's the matter? Where did Nitskee go?"

Calpurnia fixed her woeful gaze on Tom, and for a moment a look of contempt swept over her face, but then it passed and her visage softened and she sighed, with a look of long-suffering patience, and said, "Nitskee is dead."

These words sent a cold shiver over Tom's body. A ghost? He started and sent a sharp look at the woods into which Nietzsche's ghost had disappeared – he could see nothing.

"I would never have guessed ... the greatness ... the suffering ... the beauty." She sniffled, and passed her hand across her face, wiping away the falling tears, then whispered, "He called me his ... Klein Jungfer."

Tom was overwhelmed by pity for his friend; he leaned over and extended his arm over her shoulders and pulled her close to hug her, saying, "Oh, Calpurnia, I'm so sorry."

She released an outburst of small heaving sobs and let him pull her in, saying, "His Klein Jungfer ... Klein Jungfer!" She wept for a little while into Tom's side, Tom patting her back sympathetically. Tom shivered in the increasing cold, thinking it would soon drop to the point where tears freeze. Finally Calpurnia pulled herself away violently, and cried, "No! I can't take it! It hurts too much! I can't take it ..." She brought her hands up to her face and began sobbing convulsively, sometimes shaking the driver's seat with an especially violent lovepainspasm. She leaned forward onto the railing in an attitude of utter despair, and said, "We need to go back."

"Go back?" Tom asked in surprise.

"Yes!" she said between sobs and gulps and hiccups, "Go back ... uhuck ... to the redbrick house ... ahaw ... and I need to teach you that trick ... to make the pain go away."

Tom didn't even want to think about going back to the redbrick house: all he saw was bricky darkness beside more darkness, with an extreme utter darkness just down the road, moving outwards, expanding darkness, outwardpooling blackness like a flood of black ink. "I ... don't think that's such a good idea."

"Shut up you goddamn idiot! We *have to!*"

Tom suddenly realized that he was being selfish: Calpurnia was in pain, and she had done much, so much, for him; in fact, he owed her everything he had, and were it not for her he would probably be stuck back there right now anyway. But all that aside, Tom was terrified of the idea of going back. Nonetheless, he said, "All right, Calpurnia," fear breaking through his voice with little crackles.

Calpurnia sniffled and wiped her face with the short yellow sleeve of her right upper arm, and then she took a hold of the reins, her back still hunched, and managed by utilizing the two shoulders of the highway to get the carriage turned around by having the horses do a loop; then she prompted them on, back towards the town.

They rode on in silence, Calpurnia sniffling now and then, and Tom could see her shivering. At one point Tom told her she should put her jacket on, but she dismissed his suggestion with a shake of her head and said nothing. The valley was black except for the yellowywhite sparkles on the wide snake of the river, and Tom could not make out the town which he knew lay ahead. He did not like the turn things had taken: Calpurnia was greatly distraught, tormented by her hopeless love for dead Nietzsche, and the only way to solve this dilemma was to go right into the very heart of the darkness, unnamed unthinkable danger, in search of piano. He didn't know what to expect, and he didn't even want to begin considering the possibilities. He thought maybe the only way out was to bail, but he knew that he would not do this, simply because it was, even for him, unthinkable to let Calpurnia go back there alone. Thus he sat silently, waiting for the horses to drag them back to the town, expecting at every moment to meet that which cannot be expected.

They passed by the few houses which they had passed earlier from the opposite direction, and Tom knew that they were approaching the outskirts of the town. Looking down, Tom noticed that he had dropped the half-eaten sandwich in fright when he had seen Nietzsche's ghost and it had landed on his lap, leaving a streak of mayonnaise on his blue jacket: he picked it up and began hastily finishing it off, though he was not really hungry; he thought maybe the bear meat would help him, perhaps warm him, perhaps give him courage. Then suddenly Calpurnia cried "Whoah" and Tom's heart nearly leapt out of his chest in shock, and the last bit of the sandwich flew out of his hand, for his first thought was that they had come upon another ghost, or something much worse. But he could not see anything on the road ahead or on the sides of the road, squint as he might. Tom looked at Calpurnia to his left. She was staring straight ahead, in a similar attitude as that which she had had when she had seen Nietzsche's ghost, and Tom was filled by another little rush of panic and he scanned around again, but there was still nothing ahead.

Tom asked, "Calpurnia, what is it?"

Calpurnia said nothing for a while, and Tom waited patiently. Then after a time she straightened her spine and turned towards Tom and looked at him straight in his eyes, no longer crying, and said slowly and deliberately, "My love for Frydish Nitskee was the greatest thing in my life – *is* the greatest thing in my life. It is my inspiration, my rush, the only thing that makes this life worth living." She looked sharply up at the sky, moved by her words; after a time, she added, more softly, "And I am his Klein Jungfer."

She stared up at the sky silently for another few moments; then she turned her head back towards Tom, a look of solid certainty in her eyes, and said, "I can't just *erase it*, like a child, like a coward, like a ... a ..." she trailed off and bit her underlip and looked away again, her shoulders straightened decisively. She pulled the brown jacket over her shoulders, and then she took the reins and had the horses do another turn, and they began going back again along the highway away from the town. Tom was extremely relieved.

Before long they were once again at the bridge where they had seen Nietzsche's ghost at the side of the road. They went right past the spot where he had emerged from the dark woods, and Calpurnia shot a quick side-glance thereat before turning her focus once more towards the road as they crossed the bridge. Tom could see over the steel railing of the bridge a steep gorge below them, the river at the bottom invisible in the dark and possibly dry, and it went rightwards, a smaller tributary of that larger river which snaked its way westwards, now further away, at their right. Once over the bridge, the road kept sloping gradually upwards, at a gentle angle, into a dark forest-crested hill that grew against the sky ahead of them. The wind intensified, the air became gradually colder, and the temperature fell below freezing; there was not a cloud in the sky. The cold was cosmic: nothing but cold distance between them and the moon, to the far off stars whose heat died somewhere out there. A black ocean of invasive cold, smothering the insufficient starfire everywhere: endless space in which to freeze and drift alone. Supernova: a glorious death, last efforts all for nothing, never even nearly. Tom took the toque out of his jacket pocket and put it on his head, and cupped his hands over his nose and mouth to protect them from the biting wind.

When they reached the top of the hill a new view was revealed in the west: to their right, in the north, their river stretched from the east and widened and met a much larger river, that curved broadly its way southwestwards where it widened and flowed into the pool of a huge bay that spread into the southern horizon; around the bay and the river, to the north and west, rolled low round forested hills, their soft roughness dark and hidden, into the horizon; to the south, piercing through the lazy round hills, loomed the foot of a tall mountain range, jutting suddenly out of the land on the east side of the bay and rising steeply into the sky, filing like a crowd of hooded wanderers, or bandits, away into the southern horizon to the east of the bay. A long thick pillow of cloud was rolling in from the west, a row of soft grey boulders, and a frigid west wind, hitherto deflected by the hill, hammered them at full force, causing Tom to object vocally.

They went on down the road into the valley for a distance, the road heading towards the bigger river to the south of where it was joined by their river, and then soon enough Calpurnia stopped at a crossroads. On the northwest corner of the crossroads there was an abandoned gas station nestled amid the tall trees, which were beginning to obstruct the view of the valley to the right and left of the road, and dead traffic lights hung like gibbeted pirates' bodies.

Tom looked at Calpurnia, wondering why she had stopped; she was already looking at him, the same look of conviction in her eyes, and she said, "I am going to the mountains. I am taking the carriage with me, as you are incompetent. Don't worry; there is a bus that comes here" – she pointed towards a bus shelter in front of the gas-station – "that will take you to the bay, or the castle, or wherever you want to go."

Tom was about to question her, but she raised her hand, showed him her open palm, and said, "There is no other way. I must find my destiny now. Maybe one day we will meet again, when I will be a different Calpurnia and you will be ... a ... Tom." She paused and looked westwards between the shoulders of the trees at the blackness of the valley; then she turned her eyes again on Tom and continued, "Suche die Höhen: that's what he said to me."

"Sooka dee hayen?"

"Seek the heights," she said dreamily. "You know, the mountains, that kind of thing. That's where I'm going: I'm going to the mountains," – she pointed southwards – "so I'm taking a left here. You can come if you want," – she looked at Tom doubtfully – "but it won't be very much fun, and you won't like it."

Tom didn't think this was a good idea; he said, "Calpurnia, I don't think that's a good idea."

Calpurnia replied, looking away, "It's okay, Tom. There is a bus that comes here. Goodbye."

Tom slowly slid away from Calpurnia, looking at her in disbelief as he moved away from her: she was looking up at the sky, and did not turn her head as he climbed down off the driver's seat. As his feet touched the pavement the carriage slowly began to move: it moved forward about five meters and then began to turn leftwards, southwards, and Tom caught a last glimpse of Calpurnia's small form atop the carriage as it pulled away up the southbound road. The carriage shrank away and disappeared up the road into the night. Tom stood for a moment and looked up the dark road after Calpurnia. Then he looked up at the stars. He stood up on his toes and craned his neck back, losing his balance, regaining it, and then he stood for as long as he could on his toes, the stars twinkling in the immense uberblackness of space.

He finally brought his heels back down onto the pavement, shrugged, and turned towards the bus stop behind him. It was a glassy box with a low bench inside. The gas station standing to the left of it was abandoned, its windows boarded and its paint mostly peeled. He walked over and entered the bus stop and sat on the bench, facing towards the south into which Calpurnia had vanished.

Tom wondered how long it would take for the bus to arrive. Looking around he saw a bus schedule plaque behind his head; he rose and turned to read it:

> *The Bus arrives only*
> *when the time is right,*
> *and not a moment*
> *earlier or later.*

Hmm, thought Tom to himself, When the time is right?

He sat down again and looked through the glass. The glass was smeared by grey streaks, dried streams of grime. The crossroads was desolate: the thick forest encroached from every direction, making Tom feel like he was in the middle of nowhere, as if this place was here only for passing and not for stopping. He hoped the bus would come soon, for it was getting colder by the minute.

Time passed, and Tom grew impatient. He shivered in his jacket, and put the toque on; he shoved his hands in the front pockets of his jacket and stared shivering at the floor of the bus stop. After a time it began to snow, but Tom did not immediately notice because he was staring, increasingly coldly, at the concrete floor of the bus stop, his legs bouncing up and down in an effort to keep his body warm. He hoped Calpurnia was not mistaken about the bus. How unusual for her to take off like that! He wondered if she would regret her decision; he knew he did.

Tom looked up and saw, to his surprise, that a four-inch layer of snow had fallen on the ground and on the trees, whitening the night, and the sky was covered by snowclouds, hiding the light of the stars and the moon. The clear pristine light of the sky had been replaced by the duller white light of the thickly, softly falling snow. The snowflakes were large and zigzagged back and forth hypnotically, falling lightly through the dark and gathering in a fluffy blanket, drawing the gaunt skeletons of the trees and quietly burying the hidden irregularities of the dirty pebbly ground: the ceiling of sky gently collapsing to behold itself from below.

Then suddenly a strong white light flashed over the trees and through the snowflakes from behind. Turning, Tom saw about a hundred meters behind him that a tall city bus with dimly lit windows and bright headlights was driving up towards the bus stop from down the northbound road. Tom stood up and walked out of the bus stop onto the snowy sidewalk to ensure that the bus driver would not drive by without noticing him. As the bus approached he waved his left hand, and the bus slowed, causing him relief. He hoped the bus was heated, and he thought it probably was because the inside was lit.

The bus stopped with its door right before him, and the door swung open and the inside of the bus lit up with bright yellow. The whole thing was very friendly and welcoming. There were two tall steps, in the usual fashion, and the bus driver was politely invisible in the shadows behind the wheel. Tom climbed up the steps into the bus, noting to his delight that it was well heated. He stopped for a moment before the shadowed bus-driver, thinking about fare, but the driver raised a small whitegloved hand and pointed with his thumb to the wall behind his seat where a sign said FREE FOR HOLIDAYS – MERRY CHRISTMAS! Tom thanked him emphatically and sat three seats down the aisle, facing inwards with his back against the right side of the bus. The door swung shut with a rubbery slurp, the ceiling lights dimmed to a weak dark orange, and the bus began to move.

- 17 -
The Visit

The bus turned right onto the westbound road which headed into the valley. Tom could see his own reflection looking down at him in the inwardslanting window across: all he saw was a dark shape on the seat. The snowflakes whizzed by through the darkness behind his reflection. Looking around, Tom saw that the bus was empty except for the bus driver hidden in the shadows at the front of the bus on the far side of the big compartment – a closet or part of the bus' engine – behind his seat on which was pasted the generous sign.

Tom's eyes wandered, and fixed on the seat to his left; something unexpected was lying there: a bottle of dark brown liquor (whiskey, but Tom did not know this). The label was yellow and had a colourful picture of a white cottage on the waterside, surrounded by tall lush trees. Tom picked up the bottle and looked more closely at the label; it had handwriting drawn across it, but it was too small to be read. The bottle seemed to glow; it even seemed to dance. It was a very welcoming bottle, and it felt warm somehow; it seemed to emanate heat. The bus was warm, but Tom was still cold from his wait in the bus stop. Without even a second thought, Tom opened the cap on the whiskey bottle, brought it to his mouth and raised its butt so that a mouthful poured in between his lips. The taste was strong, mordant, and it made him wiggle and exclaim, "Oh!" It warmed him up. Noticing this, Tom quickly gulped another mouthful. This second mouthful made him feel dizzy almost immediately, and very warm, and he made another little surprised sound and slowly brought the bottle out in front of him with his hand, swaying with the motion of the bus, and tried to focus on the handwriting on the label again. Everything seemed to be moving more slowly. Strangely, the label seemed different now: the yellow paper was darker, and the cottage drawn on it seemed drearier, less inviting, greyer, and the trees were leafless and snow covered the ground. The handwriting was bigger. Then Tom heard a scratchy voice from the front of the bus:

"Nothing like a wee bit of the good stuff to warm ye up on a cold winter's night."

Tom thought the scratchy voice sounded familiar, but he was still trying to focus on the label, perplexed by the change he saw there. He tried to read the handwriting, but was having trouble despite its increase in size.

"I made it meself; you're welcome to it. Merry Christmas." The bus driver had a strange accent.

The road began to flatten; suddenly, the writing on the label came into focus and Tom saw that it read *Mac Murchada's Best.*. The middle word seemed somehow familiar, but Tom could not think from where exactly. It made him think of Ronny, and walking through the woods: talking with Ronny while walking through the woods. Ronny was a funny kid, Tom thought to himself, but he's probably dead now. That's not funny.

Tom felt warm and slightly drunk and a little hungry. After a few moments he said, "Thanks, I appreciate it. Merry Christmas to you too."

"Do you know where you're headed?"

Tom thought the voice was familiar. He asked, "Do I know you?" He took another swig from the bottle.

"As a matter of fact, that's a funny story, sir. We met earlier, but didn't get a chance to be properly introduced. My name is Donald Mac Murchada and I have something I need to talk to you about. Why don't you come with me to my cottage and we can have a proper chat over a snack and a drink? We can build ourselves a nice fire in the living-room. Why not, now? Come on: I've got some important information which would be good for you to hear."

The whiskey was affecting Tom's judgment. This dwarf is not such a bad character, he thought. The warmth in his belly made him feel safe, like nothing bad could happen to him, and the dizziness emboldened him. This little man is all right, thought Tom. I will have to tell Peter at some time that everybody has been misunderstanding the poor fellow entirely. "All right," Tom giggled, "Go on. You've talked me into it!"

The bus stopped slowly and very smoothly, and Donald rose into the corner of Tom's eye. Turning his head Tom saw that Donald was standing at the front of the bus; he had a brown coat on, and he was holding his top-hat in his left hand. He was taller than he had been earlier, and Tom saw that he was wearing tall platform shoes, doubtless to help him reach the pedals of the bus. He put his top-hat on and picked up a scarf which was hanging behind his seat next to the sign and wrapped it around his neck. He turned and began walking back towards Tom. He was not so ugly after all, just a little rough about the edges. He was certainly far from good-looking; there was a displaced heaviness which seemed to ooze just under the skin, barely perceptible, occupying different locations on his bones according to its fancy, never settling like the shadow of a cloud moving over a field. His beard was thicker than it had been earlier, and his moustache was almost as large as Nietzsche's had been. His eyes were shaded under the brim of his top-hat. He was not emanating the strong unpleasant aura, or the dingy pungent smell, by which Tom had been so put off earlier; however, he did smell like he owned many cats. The orange light of the bus was weak, and Tom's head was fuzzy from Mac Murchada's Best.

Donald stopped in front of Tom and extended his whitegloved hand; his head was level with Tom's. Tom took Donald's hand and shook it and Donald said, "I'm a leprechaun. Don't ask me where my gold is; the whole world is my pot of gold, and I defend it with my life. Won't you join me in my cottage down the road for a chat?"

"Nice to meet you; I've never met a leprechaun before," replied Tom.

Tom stuffed the whiskey bottle into the inside pocket of his long blue coat and followed the leprechaun down the aisle. Donald turned the key so that the engine stopped and the lights went out and pulled it out of the dashboard and put it in his pocket, and then he pulled the bus door open and stepped off the bus, Tom following him, and shut the door behind Tom. The snow had stopped falling, but the sky was still overcast. They were next to a huge bay, its waves heaving hissingly against the beach about fifty meters to the left of the road. The bay was vast and dark, and Tom could not see the horizon beneath the heavy grey clouds; it blended into the distance. Tom followed Donald down the road a short way, and then the leprechaun led him down a path that turned down towards a small cottage which Tom could barely distinguish from the trees that stood around it. Tom's shoes were getting wet from the layer of snow, but it did not bother him because of the warm glow in his belly created by Mac Murchada's Best.

Donald opened a little front door, a few inches shorter than Tom, and Tom followed him inside. Donald struck a match and lit a candle and led Tom past a small dinner table into the next room. Several cats moved around in the peripheral darkness, their eyes flashing like gems. Tom heard Donald say, "The Missus has gone to see her people for Christmas. Please excuse the mess."

"That's okay," said Tom as Donald lit another two candles, one on a shelf to the right of the doorway and another on the mantlepiece of a brick-framed fireplace in the far wall. They were in a small cozy living-room, sparsely furnished with just two normal-sized upholstered armchairs, which seemed too big to have gotten into the room through the door, sitting largely in the middle of the room facing towards the fireplace, a small coffee-table between them, a bookshelf against the wall through which they had entered at the right of the doorway, and a tiny desk against the wall to the left of the doorway. There was a closed closet in the right wall.

Donald went over to the fireplace and used his candle to light some paper under a little house of kindling, saying, "I always get the fire built before I leave every morning, so I don't have to build one in the cold."

"How sensible."

The fireplace was completely ablaze in a number of seconds, illuminating the small room: the walls were wooden and a few small paintings hung on the walls; one was a picture of some cliffs above the ocean, and Tom could see that another was a painting of a town in the mountains seen from above. Donald stood and took off his top-hat and his scarf and threw them into a corner and turned to Tom and asked, "Can I take your coat?"

Tom took off his long blue jacket and removed the whiskey bottle from the inside pocket and handed the jacket to the short figure standing before him; Donald disappeared into the kitchen through which they had entered and in a moment he was back in front of Tom and he said, "Please, sir, have a seat before the fire, won't you? It's bloody freezing out there."

"Thanks," said Tom, and he went over to the armchair on the left and sat down and began taking off his wet shoes. When he was done taking his shoes off, Donald took them and placed them in front of the fire, and then went over to the other armchair and sat and said, "Are you hungry?"

Tom thought about this. He was not starving, but neither was he devoid of hunger. He said, "I'll think about that. No thanks for now."

"Grand. I'll cook up some torture pie in a little while perhaps."

"That sounds good; thanks."

Donald chuckled happily to himself. Then for a while the two sat in silence, watching the flickering flames before them: red, orange, yellow and white, mesmerizing fire. After a few minutes, Tom heard Donald say, in an enraptured tone, little more than a whisper, "It seems to me, sir, that it's a beautiful world."

Tom said nothing, but took a large swig out of his bottle.

"You know, I wrote a poem on that very subject earlier today," continued Donald, still in his enraptured whisper. "Would you like to hear it?"

"Okay," said Tom, considering another swig.

Donald took a deep breath, and said, in a formal tone, but still a whisper,

"The highest leaf is snatched away by the breeze,
And the too bright star too soon is dwarfed.
Happier is the leaf held lower by its tree;
'Twill find itself the later turfed.
My joy doesn't wither like a rose 'neath the clock,
A towering view hinged on a fickle door.
But 'tis a landloving stream that flows over rock;
Willed downhill, my joy knows no more.
My joy is not a cloud blown fast across the sky,
No sooner spotted than banished afar.
Speedy eagle, wings spread wide up high,
Would be jealously caught and preserved in a jar.
Like a cool mist lingering lower,
The better joy moves far slower.

"What do ye think of that, eh?"

"I wish I could say I'd been as productive."

Donald chuckled, flattered, and said, "Hoho, thank ye kindly."

There was silence for a while. Tom could sense a particular tension from Donald's direction, as though he had something more to say; he heard him shifting in his seat, the soft rustle of cloth; finally Donald said, "To digress a little, are you familiar with a certain little tome called *Portentus Stomachi?*"

Tom, spurred by the sparks of recognition, "You know, as a matter of fact I've heard a lot about that today. Is it any good?"

"A bunch of Latin crap written in the future tense. It takes forever to get to the point and the author must have been a very sad prophet indeed. You won't believe me if I tell you that you yourself are something of a main character?"

"I've already been told that twice today."

"I quote from memory, translated by yours truly: 'Tom's Monster of the Stomach,' as I put it, 'will be born on an October evening. It will tear its way out of the womb with a premature appetite and devour everything it comes across. It will eat every man, woman and child, every animal, bird, tree and blade of grass in the valley. Then it will move on to the next valley, and the next valley, until it gets to the ocean, growing with every meal. Then it will turn and eat its way back through every valley, swallowing every river, until it gets to the ocean. Then it will turn and eat its way back through every valley, swallowing every river, growing with every meal, until it gets to the ocean. It will take a nap and then turn and eat its way through every valley, swallowing every river, until it gets to the ocean. It will eat every man, woman and child, every animal, bird, tree and blade of grass until it gets to the ocean. It will eat until there is nothing left and when there is nothing left it will go up the nearest mountain and eat every man, woman and child and every plant which has managed to escape it down below. It will come back down the other side of the mountain, eating everything in its path, and then it will do the same to every mountain until all the mountains are stripped, and then it will drink every river dry and follow the dry riverbeds to the ocean. It will reach the ocean and find that there is nothing left, and then it will turn back inland in search of more. When there is nothing left on the continent of America it will begin to eat its own feces. When it runs out of energy, it will collapse.' What do you think of that, now?"

That's why it was all so wrong, thought Tom to himself. He looked at Donald, wrongness oozing out of his face. "I think that sounds pretty awful. And that thing was born how long ago?"

"It doesn't matter. It has eaten many meals by now."

Tom looked around at the wooden walls of the living room, imagining the Monster breaking through with a ravenous appetite, or pulling the cottage up off its foundations and eating it in a single mouthful.

"So, Tom. I'm sure you'll understand that it is my duty to put an end to the problem right now once and for all. The world, as I told you, is my pot of gold, and you know what leprechauns do with their pots of gold."

Tom said nothing, wondering how on earth this dwarf was planning on protecting his pot of gold.

"We protect them, so we do."

"Of course," said Tom; he took a gulp of Mac Murchada's Best. "How are you planning on doing that?"

"There's a certain technique, you see," said Donald, moving back towards the wall behind Tom's chair. "It just so happens that a particular manipulation of a certain vertebra results in a complete canceling effect of the creature's existence, would you believe it? Including the existence of its offspring, and its offspring's offspring, including every meal, no less."

"Well, do what you've got to do. Wait a minute ... why don't we leave the continent instead?"

"That's a terribly irresponsible attitude to take towards me pot of gold, sonny."

Tom heard a roaring noise behind him, and he looked around the tall back of his armchair to see that the dwarf was lifting a peculiar kind of tool which looked like a thick four-foot-long screw attached to a complicated engine at its base; the screw was spinning rapidly like a drill. The noise was loud, but Tom could hear Donald's voice, "Would you please lie facedown on the floor? I promise it won't hurt a bit."

Tom did not believe him, but he was in an obliging mood, so he got up and prepared to lie down on his stomach, but then, to his great surprise, the floor began to shake wildly, and the paintings fell off the walls, and little bits of plaster fell from the ceiling. The noise of Donald's strange machine was quickly drowned out by a much louder roar, a deafening roar like that of ten atomic bombs detonated simultaneously. It was another earthquake. The last thing Tom heard before his perception shut down was Donald's cry, faintly behind the tremendous roar, "Bejasus!"

- 18 -
The Last Return

Tom awoke, like so many other times, on the belly of that fearsome Thing. Was that what it was? Yes, that was what it was. The understanding screeched over his head like a fleet of airliners. The stuff, scattered across every corner of the desert, was the offal, the deposit, the digested and redigested stuff of the world, the chewed degenerated dreams, the rejected remainder of the beauty that once was known. The Thing had eaten it all, and when there was no more to eat, ate it again, and again, and again; and, finally, when no longer able to sustain its monstrous muscleless cannibalizing bulk, it had collapsed and bleated like a crippled lamb, and was fed again and again the empty dust of dreams by he who had created it, long ago?

Tom rolled over, "Shut up. It's over now."

A fevered utterance from the belly, a chamberful of lunatics bellowed at him their muddled commands. Bombs fell, people screamed, sirens wailed in Dresden.

"Shut up. It's over." Tom buried his head with his arms, and the Thing resumed its shaking. It threw Tom up into the air violently like a trampoline possessed by devils. Feed me. "Shut up. It is over now." The Thing abused Tom in every way it could: it tossed him around, suffocated him, squeezed him nearly to death. Feed me!

"Never!"

Whimpering: a deer thrown whining on the roadside, its limbs mangled, its loud blood flowing and splashing with the sound of a waterfall onto the broken bottle pavement.

"Never!"

With a last burst of energy, the blubber threw Tom high into the air, southwards, towards the mouth, the pink cliffs of Petra, and Tom flew like a rag-doll through the wisps, the ghosts of the devoured, heard them roar in passing, and fell between the jaws into the Thing's gargantuan cavernous mouth: last act of patrophagy: destiny.

* * *

Tom was transported immediately into a room of some kind, and he was staring directly into a large bright window of gothic style: a large, sharply arched window divided into three medium-sized windows, which were in turn divided into several smaller windows. He was blinded to the inside of the room by a sharp light in the sky beyond the window, presumably a sun of some kind, which left only the rich darkish blue of the sky beyond visible to him. The light was not harsh enough to cause him to squint or shut his eyes as he would in real life; his eyes remained wide open as he stared at the sky beyond the window.

He was standing, and he continued to stand there for a long moment as he gazed contentedly at the window. The sight gave him a powerful feeling of elation, and the rays of the sun made his nerves tingle happily. Though he knew he was standing, he felt very much as though he were floating, or swaying effortlessly like a sail in a calm but steady wind. Eventually he began to drift towards the window, out of a natural and unconscious urge to have more light, more sky. He approached it slowly, surefooted, still oblivious to the room itself; he felt as though he was being pushed gently towards the window by a lukewarm wind. As he approached the window, the sky beyond opened up to him. There were soft white cumulus clouds, friendly plumy poofs not heavy enough to gather shadow in their bellies, drifting steadily across the sky. The sun was fantastic, filling the sky with brilliance and wonder and promise. It hovered low, but Tom had the strong impression that it was morning, for there was no hint of melancholy in the air – all was brightness and elation.

- The End -

February 2011

13044583R00072

Made in the USA
Charleston, SC
13 June 2012